Dennis & Cath

fm

Shane

Xmas   1995

WATERS
of the
WILD SWAN

WATERS
of the
WILD SWAN

JIM CRUMLEY

JONATHAN CAPE
LONDON

The author would like to thank Brian and Barbara Cadzow for their invaluable help, and for all they have done for swans. Thanks also to Duncan and Linda Williamson, Sheila Mackay, Tessa Ransford and Terry Williams.

First published 1992
© Jim Crumley 1992
Jonathan Cape, 20 Vauxhall Bridge Road, London SW1V 2SA

Jim Crumley has asserted his right under the Copyright, Designs and Patents Act 1988 to be identified as the author of this work

The excerpt from *Ring of Bright Water* by Gavin Maxwell is reprinted by kind permission of Penguin Books

A CIP catalogue record for this book
is available from the British Library

ISBN 0-224-03282-8

Printed in Great Britain by
Butler & Tanner Ltd, Frome and London

To my mother

Contents

Illustrations

Early whoopers caused conflict for the mutes
A pair of whooper swans feeding
The loch mutes with their cygnet
Remains of their third nest with four infertile eggs
Loch Eye – 'city of swans'
Just a swan at twilight

Mute Swans in the Dark

There is a fold down the back
of a well assembled swan
which delineates in the dark
sharp as horizons. Swans lose nothing
of whiteness in darkness
but gather mysteries.

Ducks sidle two-dimensionally by.
Moorhens merely merge. Not swans.
That spinal fold breathes breadth,
not enough to convince
but just enough to unhinge
my old preconception of nature's night

– that no bird crosses the darkness
undimmed.

I

Feathered Glory

I CHECKED IN THE MIRROR. The driver behind was dithering. Ahead
was a double-parked supermarket delivery van unloading frozen
heart disease by the hundredweight. From my parking space I could
see a fragment of clear road ahead of the van through a gap the width of
a lamppost. I gave it several seconds of hard scrutiny, then I went
decisively. The dithering one was indignant but nothing worse. I
swung out past the van, the manœuvre taking me far on to the wrong
side of the road. It was then that I saw the least predictable traffic hazard
I have ever encountered in twenty-five years of driving. Coming to
meet me, and occupying the entire width of the street and much of the
pavement as well, was a level flight of eight mute swans.

I braked, a ridiculous thing to do in the circumstances as they were
flying past the second storey windows of the street's tenement walls,
but I braked anyway. I also stopped and got out of the car in the
middle of Edinburgh on the wrong side of the road, just as the car
behind slid into my back bumper while the driver was looking at the
sky.

The swans slanted up towards the traffic lights, crossed the rooftops,
and were gone in a high banking curve. The ditherer was out of his
car too. The delivery van driver stood as frozen as his merchandise.
Half a dozen pedestrians stood mesmerised. The van driver said:

'Did you ever see anything like that *in your life*?' – and his voice rose
so high at the end of his question that it was in danger of passing
beyond auditory range. A bus hooted. A traffic warden appeared.

'Trouble?'

I looked at the ditherer, who shrugged and shook his head.

13

'No trouble,' I said, 'no trouble at all. We were watching the swans,' I added, as though that explained everything.

'Do you realise your tax disc is out of date?'

'What? – '

'Your tax disc. It's a month out of date.'

And with that he wrote out a ticket, and instead of handing it to me, plastered it to my windscreen with a yard of sellotape.

I tried to appeal to the charity in his soul. Did the sight of the swans not brighten his day? Did it not bring a touch of the phenomenal into his lousy job?

'Swans? I didn't see any swans.'

Traffic wardens have no souls. Or if they do, they are no-parking zones for charity and wild swans.

I wanted that street to celebrate the visitation of swans, but instead there was a surly snarl on the face of the traffic warden, the bus driver was leaning on his horn, the ditherer was back in his car and disentangling our bumpers, the frozen van driver had thawed out and gone about his business and the pedestrians had ambled off about theirs. I drove away suppressing rage when I should have been commemorating an astounding gesture of nature.

The commuter crawl into Edinburgh from the east offers one diversion which must be unique among the commuting journeys of the land. An alternative to the main drag is to sneak into the tenement canyon I have just mentioned, and which at its western end negotiates a mini-roundabout then explodes into the great saving grace of all Edinburgh – the miniature mountain landscape of Holyrood Park and Arthur's Seat. At the foot of the mountain lies St Margaret's Loch, a small one-time boating pond which now plays host to anything up to eighty mute swans and three or four times as many geese and lesser fowl. Because the place is so close to the centre of the city, it is quite common to see swans in ones and twos and skeins crossing high above the rooftops, or flying round the mountain to the wilder scope of a nature reserve at Duddingston Loch, or across the city to the firth of Forth. So that explains the proximity of swans to the street of my head-on encounter. It does not explain why the swans were flying down the street instead of high above it, and no amount of puzzling has produced a solution.

For all my swan-watching hours over many years, I had not, to answer the van driver's question, seen anything like it, and the impact of the moment still remains among the most durable of all my swan souvenirs. Its effect stemmed, as always with swans, from its setting, for although swans impose themselves utterly on their surroundings, the nature of the stage they strut or swim or swan-fly (a different and more glorified motion than all other forms of wild flight) transforms them uniquely. An enclosed setting – a pond, a canal, a tree-dark river – confers an air of suppressed tension on a swimming swan like an exquisitely wrapped coiled spring, or an almost intimidating authority on a flying one. A bland open setting – a large flat field where wintering swans graze in flocks – creates an illusion of something exotically oriental, brilliant imposters in the drab world of sheep. A wild Highland setting accords swans their due, perfection in nature.

But this street was none of these. It was grey and narrow and high-walled and dull and dourly urban. The swans appeared and disap-peared like a thin sheet of flame, a horizontal fork of lightning, so vivid was their sheen, so un-street-like their whiteness. The strictures of the street magnified everything – their size, which is never anything less than impressive, their bulk, their power, their grace, their sound (for the least mute thing about a mute swan is the beat of its wings, like the constantly interrupted harmonic whine of a humming top). They were so out of their element that, for the only time in my life, I caught a sense of menace in the birds' attitude. It was perhaps that, as much as the traffic warden's surliness, which so angered me as I drove off, for to interpret even momentarily the troubled flight of swans as something vindictive seemed suddenly a betrayal of all I had sought out and thought I had learned among swans. Such aggression as that flight of swans may have held would be due to the fact that the birds themselves found their surroundings menacing, that whatever fluke of mischance propelled them into that hostile grey-walled funnel, they would view their predicament with something between distaste and panic. All this I realised later, but by then my anger had fuelled the imagery of the encounter, and its surreal qualities had begun to make nonsense of logic. In a dream, days later, the swans landed on my car (an amazing feat of balance, eight swans on a Fiat Panda) and peered down inside every window while I drove on, blindly navigating the mini-roundabout, the park gates, and coming to a halt by the swans' loch with no bird in sight but two prim swimmers eating demurely from the hands of children. The car was smothered in feathers, the first in all the world's many variations of the legend of the swan-maiden to feature the internal combustion engine. If you immerse yourself in swans and their world, it is more than natural history you take on.

My addiction to swans is symptomatic of a craving for theatre-in-the-wild. My nature-writer's instincts are best served in the company of those wildlife tribes which tread a wild stage for a living, and which dominate that stage utterly with lives imbued by dramatic gesture. Eagles and ospreys and otters do it. Swans do it better because they are bigger, brighter, more willing to 'perform' blatantly and at close quarters, and they fit more perfectly my crude definition of wild beauty. True, the theatre of swans is often of a *Waiting-for-Godot*-ish nature, such is their capacity for doing almost nothing for hours on end, but I am enthralled by the perpetual expectancy of the moment which unleashes the grand gesture.

Besides, swans never do absolutely nothing. They impart a measured natural grace to even the most mundane actions, apart from walking: on dry land, especially with their wings flexed or spread wide, they look like beached Sunderland flying boats and the wonder is that the thing could ever get off the ground. Even in a one-footed doze, the bird's uncannily redesigned contours look more tense than restful, packed with possibilities. One black eye blinks restlessly open, regards me from the depths of the bird's spine (which is where it happens to have laid its head), assesses, flickers closed and reopens; apart from wind-worried feathers the eye is all in the bird that moves. But at any moment, and with no code of warning I have ever been able to detect, the grand gesture is performed. The dozing bird suddenly uncoils, is swan again after the anonymity of shapelessness, unfurls the stowed scope of a seven-foot wingspan, and I marvel again at the sculpted architecture of those wings, one of nature's great works. The deepest recesses stay swathed in deep grey-blue shade like north-facing corniced corries, while sunlight blazes clear through the wings' lowest fringes, turning them flimsily translucent. As the wingspan widens, the bird rises and stretches vertically so that it expands in every direction at once. If the bird is standing six feet away from you at the time, you are forcibly impressed with how much swan there is in a single bird. On still water, the gesture reflected, the

16

spectacle of twice the bird so spreadeagled is nature designed for maximum impact, especially if the bird is facing you, in which case the sight can be as frightening as it is beautiful.

Whatever the gesture – preening, running, taking off, landing, stretching one wing along a horizontal leg, turning eggs, upending to feed, driving out a troublesome flotilla of coots, facing down an adventurous dog, a four-day-old cygnet front-pointing up its mother's back to hitch a lift, four-month-old cygnets learning to fly eight at a time – my store of wild beauties is immediately enriched, my addiction a litle more helpless.

I ply my addiction in Scotland, which means that it swithers between mute swans and whooper swans with occasional and fleeting encounters among small and aloof gatherings of Bewicks. It lurches, too, from city park and lowland farm to wildest Highlands and an island lochan on the rim of the ocean. I have threaded the waters of my wild swans into a ragged northwards journey. It is an imperfect association of landscapes and swans, because although the journey progresses roughly from a mute swan world into a whooper swan world, the birds overlap and coincide, and do so to varying degrees at different times of the year. Indeed, the progression, as I have written it, depends as much on season as it does on landscape. You could take a different journey parallel to mine, threading a different necklace of watersheets, and come to different, even opposite conclusions. So when I wander west from Edinburgh, then north-west into the southern Highlands, through Glen Dochart and Glencoe, infiltrate Kintail and Skye, then lurch idiosyncratically into Easter Ross, that is only because that way lies the route of my landscape prejudices, landscapes where I am most at ease, and where I am happiest watching swans.

All these waters, all their wild theatres, are entrancing places in their own right. If I am sometimes less than specific, it is because their secrets have often been hard won, and because at the heart of this book is a profound love and respect for the wildness of swan and landscape which I do not feel inclined to betray. None of the lochs are hard to find, many lie alongside roads, a few do not and call for a hard day's march. All of them call for discretion and patience if you are to come close to their swans. Besides, the relationship between man and swan is far from a universal love affair. Although we smother chocolate boxes and shortbread tins and matchboxes and theatres and pubs and toilet rolls and much else besides with the imagery of swans, although we celebrate them in art and literature and music, although English monarchs have called them 'royal' for a thousand years, and although the mythology and folklore of half the nations of the world embraces swans, we also ridicule them, poison them, choke them, shoot them, beat them up, strangle them, electrocute them and even crucify them. The eye of most of us beholds beauty in the neck of a swan. The eye of some of us is satisfied only when it is broken in three places. Adult swans have no natural enemies, only man, who is as unnatural an enemy as a swan could ever conceive in its worst dreams.

For man is also the friend of swans. His hospitality has often sustained them where they would otherwise have failed. He has fed them, built sanctuaries for them, healed their wounds, and in Celtic and Norse legend (and much else besides) he has even become swan, and there are few enough of nature's creatures with which he acknowledges – even in myth and fantasy – a willingness to change place. I have come close to swans without ever becoming one. I own a much diluted strain of Celtic blood and I hanker after the northlands of the world. Swans are emissaries of both, compulsive, wonder-filled, in a big-is-beautiful way, both bold and wary, familiar friend of men and Arctic-sheened shunner of men, consummation of all nature's best efforts at grace and art and (on my native heath at least) three variations on its single stupendous theme – the Bewick, the whooper, and the anything-but-mute.

The mute swan is the one we all know, the chocolate box cliché, and it is no more mute than your mother-in-law. It grunts, whistles, hisses, snorts, and in flight its wings make one of the most magical sounds in nature. The young birds peep a bit weedily, even when fully fledged and almost fully grown, by which time such a sound in such a bird is as disappointing as the thin terrier yap of a golden eagle or the reedy whistle of ospreys. The mute swan is the largest flying bird in the world. There are wider wingspans than the cob's seven-to-eight feet, but no bird with a greater overall mass. A typical weight for an average male swan is 12 kg, about 25 lb, but 15–16 kg birds turn up and occasionally, very occasionally, 18–20 kg. Such a huge bird would be unlikely in the wild. With so much flesh, it is no wonder that they were once considered an important source of food, although the darkness of the flesh beneath its beautiful white plumage once gave rise to the early Christian belief that it was the symbol of a hypocrite.

Mute swans differ from whoopers and Bewicks in several character-istics – the curve of the neck and the prominently raised tail of the mute are the most obvious at a distance, the orange bill with its round black knob of tissue at the top is the giveaway at close quarters. Males are larger than females and the black knob is more pronounced.

The whooper is a winter visitor to Britain, although occasional birds have bred in Scotland. They arrive between September and late November and most have left again by the beginning of May for the nesting grounds in Iceland. It is as large as the mute, but holds its neck straight and its tail low, and the bill is a yellow and black wedge shape. Their call is a particularly charismatic brassy bugling – vari-ations on the theme of 'woo-pah!' – loudest in flight or when alarmed. Whoopers do not have the mute swan's unique wing-song.

The Bewick swan was not discovered by the engraver and naturalist Thomas Bewick, but was named after him by William Yarrell two years after Bewick's death in 1828. Bewick may well not even have known that the species existed, because until Yarrell named it, it was still widely held to be the same bird as the whooper swan. The principal difference between the two birds is one of size – the Bewick is much smaller – and although the birds have the same wedge shape and colouring on their bills, there is much less yellow on the Bewick's. Few wintering Bewicks stay in Scotland, whereas only a small percentage of Britain's whoopers winter beyond Scotland. You may chance on small and aloof groups of Bewicks on the lochs and firths of eastern and southwest Scotland or feeding in stubble fields a discreet distance from a large flock of whoopers. They are pocket-sized swans, which seems a denial of one of the points about being a swan – the big-is-beautifulness of it all.

Yet in another sense they are the most remarkable of our swans, natives of the highest Arctic. It is when you consider the unvarnished statistics of the life cycles of the three species that crucial differences emerge. Mute swans have often courted, mated and nested before the whoopers and Bewicks leave for their nesting grounds, the whoopers for Iceland, the Bewicks for Arctic Russia. But mute swan cygnets take anything up to 150 days before they can fly. The whoopers fly after seventy days and Bewicks after forty. A mute swan cygnet which hatches in mid-to-late May will perhaps not fly until late September or early October, by which time their Bewick counterparts will not only have fledged, but also made the traumatic 2,000-mile journey back to Britain from the breeding grounds. The pace of the whooper summer is only marginally less frantic, but the lifestyle of both migrating species is assisted by 24-hour daylight and therefore 24-hour feeding. Captive birds in Britain are slower breeders, but the comparison of the three birds shows what a languid start to life a young mute swan makes. There is a correspondingly long period of vulnerability among cygnets – 150 flightless days is too much risk for any wild bird, even one with such formidable guardians.

So these are the swans, and the loch under Arthur's Seat is the easiest place I know to stitch together fragments of swan behaviour, often out of season, often out of sequence, often a cameo in complete isolation from the pattern of a breeding pair's life-cycle, because it is the realm, almost exclusively, of young and non-breeding adults where anything goes, anything that is but nesting.

Thus you can see two birds enacting the violently balletic mating ritual of swans in September rather than March or April, which is when you would be more likely to see a breeding pair doing it. What happens then is that the spectacle excites other swans on the loch and twenty or thirty more birds might try to join in, a fantastic collision of breasts and necks and wingspans. It is a turbulent but largely unconsummated orgy in which the worst that can happen is that one uncertain cob will pounce on an astonished greylag goose, propel it underwater in a manner quite acceptable to mating swans, but which is rather more affection than the average goose can accommodate. So instead of the erotic submission of the pen beneath the water, there is the terrified resistance of a threshing goose hellbent on the chastity of the shore. Such a goose which grounds in the shallows with the swan reluctantly releasing its clutches is a staggering, wheezing, hysterical wreck. It immediately attracts the consoling attentions of others of its tribe while the cob backs off and returns to the fray wondering where he went wrong.

You feel for the outraged goose, and if you know your Yeats, you feel for Leda who was similarly put upon in the poet's immortal 'Leda and the Swan':

Feathered Glory

A sudden blow: the great wings beating still
Above the staggering girl, her thighs caressed
By the dark webs, her nape caught in his bill,
He holds her helpless breast upon his breast.

How can those terrified vague fingers push
The feathered glory from her loosening thighs?
And how can body, laid in that white rush,
But feel the strange heart beating where it lies?

A shudder in the loins engenders there
The broken wall, the burning roof and tower
And Agamemnon dead.
                         Being so caught up,
So mastered by the brute blood of the air,
Did she put on his knowledge with his power
Before the indifferent beak could let her drop?

Likewise, did the violated goose put on swan's knowledge and live
unhappily ever after in the twilit realm of swan-goose, or simply
shrug it off and head for swan-free waters, unmoved by the feathered
glory?

2

Sentries of the Winter Night

T HE SITUATION OF St Margaret's Loch may be tame, and although the swans will mostly take food from a human hand, they are both wild in their seasonal flights and in their characteristic behaviour. The opportunities for watching that behaviour at close quarters in an environment where swans are unwary of people should neither be scorned nor missed. Watch this pen, for example, as she swims to a half-submerged rock, clambers onto it and begins to preen. Swans like this kind of perch, possibly because it panders to an ancient need for security for the wholly absorbing and time-consuming ritual of preening. I have watched whooper swans on a lochan in Skye adopt precisely the same attitude before beginning to preen, but these were the shyest of swans newly arrived from the north, uncertain of their surroundings, unconfiding in people, and seeking out the wildest of landscape refuges. Other wildfowl, particularly mallard duck, also like a submerged preening perch, although as a spectator sport, they have none of the swans' star attractions. Preening preoccupies swans, and especially mute swans, as it preoccupies few other bird tribes. Mike Birkhead and Christopher Perrins, authors of *The Mute Swan*, provide an astounding statistic which explains why:

. . . nobody has ever counted the feathers of a mute swan but people once counted those on a whistling swan. This latter bird, which weighed 6.1 kg, had 25,216 feathers, weighing 621g, one tenth of its total weight. Presumably mute swans, some of which are twice the weight of this bird, have even more feathers.

If the implication of that equation is 50,000 feathers, the ritual which roots a single swan to the spot for an hour or more at a time, preening everything from tiny throat feathers to eagle-sized primaries, assumes a critical significance.

It is, like so much of swan behaviour, a ritual of fluid grace. The pen stands on her rock. The light has yellowed in the late afternoon and her cloak of vivid white has assumed insinuations of the changed light, and her underbelly takes on the warmer hue reflected from dark waters. With her tail whipping up a small whirlpool of circles in the water around her, she stands high and deep-chested and, her neck straighter than it will be at any time in the next hour, she tucks her bill into her throat and begins.

The neck starts to arc as she works down its length, sifting, scattering, scuffing, soothing, smoothing, smooring the white fires of her plumage back into a semblance of sublime decorum. The almost limitless flexibility of the mute swan neck begins now to extend its repertoire, as she tackles the lowest of her neck feathers and the highest of her breast. To ease the process the neck is first laid off to one side then permits two thin curves so that her bill, now pointing above the horizontal from her inverted head can penetrate deep into her breast down. With every new stage of the process, the bird's profile lowers and widens, so that by the time she has gravitated through every last contour of her own feathered landscape to the underside of her tail, she is a low-slung and barely recognisable conglomeration of curves, as far removed from the heron-like beginnings of the ritual as your imagination or a swan's physiognomy can conceive. Throughout, her balance has not shifted an inch.

What she has not done is preen the feathers on the top and back of her head, and just when you are thinking that not even a swan can do that, she takes to the water, lifts one langorous web above her back, lays her neck along her back, turns her head upside down and preens the inaccessible feathers with her foot. Good, eh?

Then she begins to bathe. Remember the blackbird in the back garden bird-bath, scattering lacy inches-wide showers across the patio? Forget it. Forget everything you ever saw about birds bathing. When a swan bathes, a small loch rises and falls and eddies under the impact. At its most boisterous the bird rolls right over, immersing everything but its underbelly and feet. Once I watched an immature mute swan immerse by forward-rolling in perfect imitation of a surrounding flotilla of diving tufted ducks. The violence of the whole process

23

seems to be fundamental to the required effect. From a distance, it looks like a rag in a gale, something out of control and motivated into frenzy by irresistible forces. There is a frantic, uncoordinated shapelessness quite uncharacteristic of every other aspect of swan behaviour. Wings thrash the water independently of each other: one is often pointing at the sky while the other is submerged, then the bird see-saws and the position is reversed. The wings can also appear to revolve like those of a slow-motion humming-bird, heaving quantities of scooped water over the bird's back. Suddenly the whole frenzy subsides and a swan shape emerges, instant smooth control. It is a lull.

Within moments a new bout erupts and a small storm of wavelets slaps the shore twenty yards away. The longest I ever timed a swan bath was forty minutes, a sustained expenditure of energy which must have left the bird more exhausted than invigorated. It was also a singularly convincing demonstration of the raw power stored in that formidable generator over which nature has drawn the thin veil of a swan's suave streamlining.

Edinburgh taught me to look for another characteristic of swans which is not obvious at a causal glance – colour. The overwhelming presence of that small mountain which all sunlight must negotiate and the fluctuations of Edinburgh's boisterous winds are forever working new tricks of light and shade on St Margaret's Loch, and that bird you perhaps always wrote off as 'white' catches every nuance of the trickery. By one of those enlightened coincidences which have punctuated my nature writer's life, and within months of first noticing the shades which rippled through a mute swan's flexed wings in a low evening sun, I encountered a passage in a book called *Bird Portraiture* by the man I hold to be the apotheosis of all wildlife artists, Charles Tunnicliffe. He dismissed the idea of a 'white' bird, and his artist's eye alighted on those properties of swan feathers which hold the influences of light and shade and tone and colour from its surroundings. For example:

> Notice the yellow tinge in the feathers of neck and upper breast, and the cold bluish purity of the back, wings and tail. Note also the colour of the shadowed under-surfaces and how it is influenced by the colour of the ground on which the bird is standing: if he is standing on green grass, then the under-parts reflect a greenish

colour, whereas if he were on dry, golden sand, the reflected colour would be of a distinctly warm tint; or again if he were flying over water, his breast, belly and under-wings would take on a colder tint, especially if the water were reflecting a blue or grey sky.

But suppose the swan is swimming ahead of you, and straight into the sun:

. . . only his upper surfaces are lit by sunlight, the rest of him being in shadow and appearing dark violet against the bright water; in fact, but for the light on his back and the top of his head he appears as a dark silhouette in relation to the high tone of the water.

Snow changes everything, and a swan in snow can look anything but white:

Now you can see how yellow his neck is, and, to a lesser extent, the rest of his upper plumage. Note also the reflected snow light on his undersides which makes them look almost the same tone as, or even lighter than, his top surfaces.

Armed with Tunnicliffe's insights into these and other landscape situations where swans find themselves, I have unearthed and divined undreamed-of colours in that bird the field guides dismiss as having 'white plumage'. Driving through the Carse of Stirling (a regular swan-watching haunt) one early spring evening with a blood-red sun at my back, I stopped to watch two mute swans cross the road ahead, then turn west to fly past me into the setting sun. They were not white birds at all but an almost incandescent orange. Yet no swan is as simple as that to colour-code, especially in flight, and as their wings stroked high and low, the orange tone seemed to flash on and off as the wings caught the full glow of the sun, then shaded themselves. But because I was watching the birds side-on, the sunlight would catch the underside of the near wing and the topside of the far wing of each bird as they flew, so that the on-off effect was multiplied by four at every stroke of the birds' wings. Through all that, the birds' backs and necks remained bright orange, their lower bodies a paler pinky white. Then a stand of trees intervened, shading one bird, but not the other, so that the fire in its plumage was smoored at once, while the other, flying three or four feet higher and as far behind, still worked

25

the on-off trick. Without Tunnicliffe, I would never have been wise to the spectacle, and might never even have paused to watch it.

People come a long way to feed the swans on St Margaret's Loch, or round the mountain at Duddingston. The particular attraction of St Margaret's Loch is the sheer number of swans, as few as a dozen in high summer, but in winter and spring anything between forty and eighty is normal. Eighty mute swans hanging on your every gesture is not a trivial experience, even if half of them wear the dowdy off-brown cloak of youth. Inevitably, too, that handsome congregation will be swelled by the native greylags and an often huge floating population of ducks – mallard, tufted, pochard, occasionally teal and wigeon, and a small plague of coots. But these are the flotsam of the loch, the bit-part players. It is the swans people come to see, and to feed, doubtless oblivious as they do so that they are the guardians of ancient tradition, an association between city and swan whose origins are at least mediaeval, and possibly older. Back in the heyday of Edinburgh's Old Town, when the Old Town was all the Edinburgh there was (a tapsalteerie rough-and-tumble of crammed living from stem to stern of the Castle Rock), the northern cliff of the rock brooded over the waters of the Nor' Loch. That loch has long since been drained to accommodate the railway and Princes Street Gardens, but for long enough it was a wild water much prized by the people on the Rock. A museum-piece model of Edinburgh in the time of Mary Queen of Scots shows the loch well patronised by pleasure boats – and swans. Reality was rather that the loch was prized in much the same way as Edinburgh now prizes its sewage works, and it was often the last resting place for the mediaeval equivalent of supermarket trolleys and dead refrigerators. The most prolific wildlife there appears to have been water rats and eels, trout and swans. Eel pie was a great tradition in the howffs of the High Street, and the sixteenth-century town council rented out an 'eel ark' on the Nor' Loch, which was a lucrative venture. But if the waters were not scrupulously maintained, it seems the swans were, and the tenant of the eel ark was required to feed the swans. The book *Castle and Town*, published in 1928, records that:

> The swans on the loch are referred to in a variety of minutes. Thus on 8th December 1589, a payment of 50 shillings is recorded for oats for the swans on the loch; and similar outlays appear in later

26

years. On 3rd December 1600, the Masters of the Trinity Hospital were required to provide a boll of oats for the swans in the coming winter. On 8th December 1589 there is an interesting reference to an individual accused of shooting a swan from a window in his house which looked out on the loch, and it is stated that other householders had indulged in this form of sport. The person referred to was taken bound to replace the swan he had destroyed and forbidden to shoot from his dwellinghouse at any kind of bird on the loch.

James Grant, whose three-volume *Old and New Edinburgh* is still the seminal work on the city, although it was produced a hundred years ago, singles out the same incident:

> For the sake of ornament the magistrates kept swans and wild duck on the loch, and various entries for their preservation occur in their accounts; and one passed in Council between 1589–94 ordained a boll of oats to be procured for feeding them. A man was outlawed for shooting a swan in the said loch and obliged to find another in its place.

The story is infuriatingly incomplete. I want to see the face of the outlaw as the magistrates intone sentence, to see it twist in fear and the sweat stand on his brow like the blood that welled on the breast of his shot swan, for I have typecast him as an insufferable coward; he too has descendants who perpetuate an ancient tradition of cruelty against swans, and I never forgot the solution of Len Baker who founded a swan hospital in Norfolk and who has seen every form of imaginable atrocity committed against swans. The punishment he would mete out is that offenders be put in a locked room with six swans.

So I see the mediaeval marksman cringe at the prospect of his punishment. Did the magistrates allow him the comparative luxury of enough time to replace the swan so that he could capture one during the flightless summer weeks of the moult? I hope not, but even then, any healthy adult swan would mount a healthy resistance to the prospect of capture. Did he succeed? Did the swan inflict vengeful injury? The minutes are silent, and we shall never know. But you see how it is when you while away your Sunday afternoon with a bag of crusts and a billowing wake of eighty swans attending your leisurely progress round the loch? And when your head is turned by a flight of swans across the city's rooftops looking like a penant flown from Edinburgh's matchless skyline, know that such birds have turned the heads of all Edinburgh's famed eras; and if your taste in sport inclines you to follow the flight along the barrel of an airgun or (a sinister fad) through the sights of a crossbow, know that there is a fearful precedent by way of punishment, which may well be embellished by Edinburgh's many swan-friends throwing you into St Margaret's Loch.

Duddingston Loch is a very different water. It lies on the other side of the mountain, the size of a small Highland loch, three of its four shores more or less inaccessible. The fourth is another favourite bird-feeding place, but here the greylag geese predominate and the air is frantic with their shouts, the screeching of black-headed gulls, the shrill oaths of hundreds of foul-mouthed coots. The swans are fewer here, although there is infinitely more room for them, but there is a resident breeding pair, and come the spring the cob stakes a territorial claim which is non-negotiable. So here is another object lesson at close quarters into the behaviour of swans, ten minutes from the heart of Edinburgh, a situation, incidentally, which makes Duddingston one of the most astonishing nature reserves in Scotland. Winter swans are a sociable tribe, seeking out each other's company, even muttering companionably with small gatherings of whooper swans in the right places (wilder waters than this), but in early spring, the swan with a territory to re-establish is a crude and intimidating brute towards all other swans, including his own young of the year before if they have lingered. A mature intruding cob is vigorously discouraged, and if he persists, the ensuing conflict can sometimes be resolved by the death of one of the combatants. Such a fight is as frightening as it is spectacular, and inexpert human intervention, even if it is possible, is unwise. The principal weapon of a fighting swan is not its beak, which is incapable of inflicting more than a graze on a human finger, but the 'wrist' joint of the forewing, a formidable club of bone which is wielded with telling power.

More often, however, the threat tactics of the cob are convincing enough, and most unwelcome birds retreat before it, doubtless in the knowledge that the alternative is to fight to the death, or at the very least to humiliation.

Swans in Edinburgh, a 500-year-old association
Mute swans entwine necks as a prelude to mating

The drama and grace of mute swans mating

The farm pond, perfect swan habitat and manmade
The pond's resident cob 'stands' to flex his wings

The pond's island nest, the pen on eight eggs

Eight out of eight!

I slip into a favourite rock perch on the lochside on a paling and misty dusk of early March, when the water is at its most seductive, all Edinburgh at my back a subdued, vast and all but invisible presence. The mute swan pair are far across the loch by its deep and carefully nurtured reed beds. The coots are squabbling interminably, the moorhens are choking on their own monosyllables. Herons drift heavily to the lochside heronry, rasping greetings. Two great crested grebes are arse-dancing, a technique of extravagant courtship ritual without visible means of support. A symbolic piece of vegetation passes from bill to bill, head and neck feathers are raised and flared, and an exchange of excited gutturals carries across the still water.

The geese are more or less becalmed, a thick raft of fifty birds just offshore, but they stir themselves to greet a small skein of a dozen late-comers. These announce their arrival to me with a thrilling rush of spilling air as they whiffle down the hill slope at my back, a controlled chaos of wings. Behind them, audible above all the honking cacophany of their arrival, the pulse of swans' wings, which the cob on the far side of the loch has already heard. Three young swans, mottled of plumage and dull-billed, land close to the geese, as doubtless they have been doing through the winter.

It had proved a safe and sociable water for a winter night, and they would have no way of knowing that in the last few days, the rules had changed, that the resident breeding pair of swans had changed them. The same companionable swans which held open house for all-comers were suddenly and passionately intolerant of the sight and sound of other swans. Two days ago, the cob had driven out the two survivors of last year's brood. Now, as the three immatures splashed down by the geese, the cob spun away from the side of his mate and set off on a quarter-of-a-mile sprint across the loch with a single-minded intent.

I put the glasses on him. He came head-on, which is the most impressive angle to observe a roused male swan, provided you are not the object of his attentions. His wings hoisted like two great mainsails, a small bow-wave appeared at his breast, then his head went ominously low almost to his own waterline, the neck marvellously withdrawn as if it had never been. The young swans suddenly sensed his approach, and if they were slow to react, it could simply be that it was the first time they had ever encountered the phenomenon and mistook its purpose. From 200 yards, he charged, wings and feet thrashing the water, neck restored and stretched low and straight, and the young swans panicked. Two of the three turned and fled, first running then flying low across the loch to a far unturbulent corner, perhaps half a mile away. The third fell foul of an intervening goose and lost valuable seconds. The big cob crash-landed in front of him, by which time he was massively filling the glasses, and his momentum converted into a high and wide-winged attack. A single blow from the 'wrist' of one wing, sent the young bird staggering from its frantic escape route, so that for a handful of chaotic yards it was a grotesquely lop-sided parody of itself, and hopelessly ill-prepared for defence. But the cob subsided onto the water, called off the assault, the point already made. He would recognise the young swan as no serious threat to his ownership of territory, and within seconds the victim was low over the water in the wake of its fellows.

The three licked their wounded pride by that far shore, but the cob was not satisfied with a partial withdrawal. Again the sails were unfurled, and with head high he launched a second pursuit, looking like a Viking longboat which had suffered from the attentions of a deranged sail-maker. Then the head lowered, wrecking the image, and the second headlong rush put the young ones to flight. I lost them high over a shoulder of the mountain, dark shapes against a purpling sky.

The pen spent all this time mooching half-heartedly behind her mate, and now turned back towards the reed bed where nest-building had begun, with cob following a hundred yards adrift, equilibrium restored.

I love to be a part of the deepening stillness of a lochside dusk, even one which has the muffled throb of a city for a backdrop. In one sense, the presence of the city enhances the impression of stillness because of the starkness of contrast between the regimes of city and nature. Owls and herons punctuated the quiet with screams and scrapes, while the geese and the coots and the moorhens bantered away at each other, the way they do, and a passing flotilla of mallards was a brief quacking choir. But still the omnipresence was one of silence. It was shattered by the emergence from the thickest reeds of the sound of a badly-tuned kettle-drum amplified through an old foghorn and belched onto the evening air with all the decorum of (this being Edinburgh) a

Grassmarket drunk. Or you can believe science if you would rather, because science has accorded the source of the sound the generic name Botaurus which has something to do with the Latin for the bellowing of a bull. I adhere to the foghorn/drum theory, but either way, I was listening to my first bittern.

It is a small miracle of this place (the big miracle being that it exists where it is at all) that for all the city sprawl of its surroundings, it has the capacity to attract all manner of vagrants and birds of passage. A bittern haunts the reed beds most winters, but you can probably count on the fingers of one hand the number of people who have seen it. I am not among them. The bird is probably big enough and loud enough to trouble the equilibrium of the swans, but only if it took to the open water. That it does not do. It's a skulker, a loner, a fly-by-night or at least by dusk, and survives daylight persecution by doing reed impersonations in a reed bed, an uncanny trick of camouflage, or so they say. I have never seen it done to pass judgment. The voice though, once heard, is not readily forgotten.

Duddingston Loch and its far shoreline of Bawsinch is managed as a nature reserve by the Scottish Wildlife Trust, an imaginative venture which not only gives pleasure to thousands of people a year but offers hospitable sanctuary to wildfowl and other bird tribes which would otherwise never dare to cross the city's frontier. And by deliberately creating a conducive habitat, they induced a handful of greylag geese to establish one of Scotland's very few breeding colonies. Now that colony flourishes. Most of all, they have put the flight of swans on the ancient skyline of the only city I ever learned to love, and for that I concede a debt of some gratitude.

Edinburgh poet and director of the Scottish Poetry Library, Tessa Ransford, doubtless acknowledges a similar debt, but for her there is more to it, for she lives cheek by the mountain's jowl, close enough and with its crouched lion silhouette filling enough of her windows to base a volume of poetry on a year in the mountain's life. Inevitably the poems of *Shadows from the Greater Hill* touch on the swans and in accordance with tradition and folklore inexplicably common to half the globe, the swans become ambassadors of the human psyche as well as that isolated fragment of nature's domain. This poem in particular intrigued:

Waters of the Wild Swan

Three swans flew westward
in the filmy, cloud-white morning,
a triangle
a threesome like an arrow.

One is the swan of ambition
another the swan of emotion
The third swan keeps the balance,
flies with cloudy, filmy patience.

The idea of a trinity of swans emblematically used to represent a complete human condition is the poet's own invention, but it bears an uncanny resemblance to the old Norse legend of the Three Nornes, in which Past, Present and Future are represented by intertwining swans. I was fascinated enough to ask Tessa Ransford about her choice of imagery. She responded by letter:

As far as the 'compost' for the swan poem is concerned, I think it was to do with my work for the Library and my family life. (Compost is how Graham Green described what goes into writing which you are hardly conscious of and later forget about.) I started working for the library in 1982 when my youngest was only eleven. Later when I was living on my own with her, in 1984 and after, she was a bit neglected because it was non-stop for me keeping the SPL going.

The arrow made by the three swans flying through filmy cloud was like my purpose for the library spearheading the flight, but its being sustained by the steadying emotion, and reason/common sense keeping the balance patiently. I wasn't consciously invoking any myths but I suppose swans do seem to reflect something of our own imagined dreams and desires. I used to look out of my window in 1985 and wonder if I was right to be giving up everything for the Library, yet knowing I had no choice. I was already in flight in that respect and to come down would have been even more disastrous for everyone.

In such a way, a life can be touched by swans. But when you have swans for neighbours, all kinds of images and analogies are at your disposal, particularly if you are a poet with a sensitivity to nature.

32

Tessa Ransford's letter contained an aside invoking the Gulf War and a second poem. She explained, 'I wrote a "note" poem comparing one flying past the window to John Simpson's Baghdad missile.' The reference was to BBC TV correspondent John Simpson, who memorably described seeing a Scud missile passing down the street in search of a target from his hotel window. The poem is called 'Passing the Window':

> Swans fly slowly past my high window
> elongated with heavy wings
> huge and white in twos and threes
> but in Baghdad a missile
> was cruising down the street
> a hundred feet high
> seen accidentally by John Simpson
> from his hotel window on the second
> night of the Gulf War. He did not know
> what it was aimed at. I have seen
> the swans fly south to find the Tweed
> where they will glide with the current
> wings raised as sails, effortless, superb.

I thought, when I read that, of my streetful of swans and wondered if they knew what they were aimed at, wondered if anyone was watching from that second storey window when a level flight of eight swans brushed past like traffic, whether they would have struck a cold sweat of familiarity in John Simpson, back from Baghdad. The idea of a swan as missile caught my imagination, self-propelled in defence of its own realm, explosive in its charge. Or perhaps a lance was better. The thought lodged and would resurface.

How often since we stopped eating swans and making hats out of their feathers, has a swan turned a human head just by going about the everyday business of being a swan, and how often borne on its wings the burden of our hopes and emotions? I have grappled many times with half-baked theories – mine and other people's – about why so many races of the world place their faiths and carve their symbolism into swan shapes, and I have found no satisfactory answer. Tessa Ransford's letter considered one possibility which had not occurred to me: 'Swans are huge. It seems impossible they can fly. It is almost like a human being in flight . . .' That notion too would resurface.

Winter nights turn St Margaret's Loch into a wilder stage. The nearby road is unlit, the mountain is a black mask, the city a source of skylighting which seems suddenly far off. The loch is hard ice, a blue-black sheen which holds the sky-bounced night light of the city like a satellite receiving-dish. Sixty-three swans are gathered here, give or take a tall-headed blur or a folded-away sleeper screened by a pale and thickening straight-necked plantation of birds where the swans have kept a pocket of water ice-free and been gatecrashed by dozens of duck. Counting swans on a small loch is difficult enough in daylight. At night, you can be a dozen out in a flock of fifty, or count the same number twice. Few birds seem to sleep for long when the cold is as intense as this. There is a perpetual stir among the swimming mass of birds. The swans continually breast the fringes of the ice, breaking it down, holding the next inch of its advance at bay. Others stand around all over the loch, curved ghosts, each bird on its own single web-footed pedestal, neck abstractly woven into the unclear mass of flank and back. Yet others rouse and walk uncertainly back to the water, to the safety of numbers, the relative warmth of the pack.

I have walked to the darkest corner of the loch to watch the soft hubbub from a distance, to stand among the one-footed ones, and find the same dark corner occupied by four mallard drakes. Disconsolate is a word invented to describe night ducks on ice. These four, with their heads turned and embedded between their 'shoulders', look like unlit Chinese lanterns suspended from beneath, or bloated sea urchins mysteriously landlocked, or . . . or . . . just about anything but ducks. Mostly, though, they look one-footed and disconsolate. They have their counterparts in the city beyond, the slouched two-footed wanderers of the darkest streets, hoping for a bed in a hostel, a doorway, or wrapped round a bottle just about anywhere. These four mallards walk the back alleys of the loch, down-and-outs for as long as winter cares or doesn't care. They move and stand again, now back-lit by the ice's glare, black ducks from a child's puzzle book.

A night like this at this time of year can mean eighteen dark hours to stand through, stare through, drowse through, hour after hour after hour of their hour-less life. Yet these are the lucky ones, for the city feeds them by day. Carfuls of Samaritans cast bread on their iced waters, and mostly, they will eat well enough to thole the nights, a fact not lost on the city fox, which lumbers up in a long contouring traverse of the mountain from a daytime refuge in the fag-end of a Duddingston garden. Nor is the fact of the ice lost on the fox. Where the ducks stand and walk, a fox can stand and walk. There are no Samaritans to feed foxes, but the city fox is a survivor. Cold and hunger are just two more hands turned against him, and they have little more impact on him than all the guns, poisons, traps, terriers and pink-jacketed poseurs and their yap-dogs have ever had on his country kin. He is a hunter, and cold and hunger merely keen his hunter's instincts and embolden him. He knows there may be a gauntlet of swans to run, and for that he would have no stomach, but he will put wary night eyes on the loch from a safe distance, and if necessary wait out as much of the night as it takes before the restless throng discards one unwary bird into a briefly exposed position of weakness.

It was 10 p.m., the city quiet, the hour marked by a distant bell whose chime wavered through the vagaries of the wind, now bright and brimming, now hesitant and muffled. Owls conversed in night screams. I threaded my way confidently up through the whins from the loch with a torch for the pitfalls, but I knew my ground. Edinburgh had a back-of-the-hand familiarity for me then, for I worked for its local newspaper, the *Evening News*, as columnist, wildlife columnist, features editor, chief features writer and leader writer, combining several of these roles at any one time. But the city I clung to, when I had the choice, was the Old Town on its rock and the mountain beyond Holyrood where the swan-descendants of the Nor' Loch thump the city winds with their wings. I threaded these whinny alleys as I threaded the Old Town closes, footsure and relishing their familiarity.

Above the nearest whins, the track dips into a hollow which shuts out the city and darkens the world at a stroke, so that only the lit sky at my back proclaimed Edinburgh's presence. In that instant, while I grappled with the new demands made on my eyesight, my path crossed the fox's, and I sensed and smelled rather than saw his grass-rattling dash. Then he was up on a higher snow slope, the legacy of last week's blizzard, and climbed swiftly upwards in an unfaltering diagonal, his moonshadow for company. Beyond the snow he stopped, regarding me over his shoulder with a clarity of vision which is exclusive to those who haunt the night for a living. My eyes struggled back, but I don't haunt enough of the night to be fluent at it. Not that I couldn't be with practice. Chris Ferris, whose mesmerising book *The Darkness is Light Enough* recounts wildlife observation at night, taught herself night vision: 'Monday 21 September. 2.25 a.m. Dull overcast night after four days and nights of storms and high winds. My visibility excellent – can see every detail of the ploughed earth, tree bark and leaves at the same distance as by daylight – only a different kind of vision.' She also quotes a *New Scientist* article about owls: 'The high similarity of owl and human visual sensitivity thresholds does not mean of course that we should regard man as a nocturnal creature, but it does suggest that our diurnal habits are not because we are any blinder in the dark than nocturnal animals.' Chris Ferris's book is a triumphant vindication of that theory.

The fox ambled away, and the last I saw of him, he was sloping down a long curve of hill that might bear him towards the loch, if ducks were on his mind. The last I saw of him, of course, doesn't mean that he wasn't still around to be seen, merely that the seeing wasn't up to seeing any more of him.

The night mountain is a quietly industrious place. The hollow was offering small sanctuary to a covey of a dozen or so red grouse (which may also have been on the fox's mind and explained his presence hereabouts) and these erupted from beneath my last stride, but with none of the cackling go-back-ing rebuke so typical of the bird in its moorland element. Here, uneasy in their stop-over accommodation, they were no more than a diminuendo of wing sounds, a softening scatter of shapes which quickly outclassed the limits of my night vision. Up there, where they flew, I know the haunt of a short-eared owl with eyes to outsmart mine, and a silent way of crossing the night air which could catch out even the uneasiest of benighted grouse.

I wandered in a wide semi-circling detour to a knoll which looks down on the loch, but also out to the city's electric blaze. Chris Ferris wrote how even a car headlight beam could disrupt the efficiency of her night vision. Now with the lit miles of Edinburgh to contend with, the loch had become a troublesome sheet of confused shadows where swans were dim ghosts and the mass of ducks as indefinable as coal in a cellar. It took twenty shivering minutes to effect a measure of readjustment. One shape detached itself from the throng, discernible more by its un-bird-like gait than from any certainty of identification. I shifted from the shape to the swans still in their peaceable huddle, rocking themselves in and out of sleep to keep a pocket of water ice-free. The shape was moving away from them, down the loch's mountain shore, stalking a scatter of one-footed duck statues strewn across the ice. I had caught up with the fox, but if I was seeing him from up here, the chances of him crossing the ice unseen by all the loch's night eyes were not good. He stepped slowly from shore to ice, and had set perhaps a dozen fox-straight paw-prints on the frosted surface when two swans lunged from water on to ice, smashing the flimsy ice fringes of their small haven to glittering splinters, and in a fury of threshed wings and ungracious uncontrolled slides, drove at the fox from fifty yards away. I have often tried since then to put myself in the fox's place.

At the sound of the first cracking of the ice under the clambering thrust of the swans' webs and breasts – or perhaps his ears were attuned enough to catch the preliminary warning hiss which invariably presages mute swan aggression – the fox would throw a fearful two-eyed stare back over his shoulder, ears craning. He would see one of the most formidable sights in nature – the uncorked wrath of two run-flying swans, the bowsprit of head and neck pointing unmistakably at him and magnifying monstrously by the moment (swans as missiles, again). The swans never really became airborne, wings threshing as much for terrorising effect as for momentum. Two wingspans, each seven-feet wide, wing-tip to wing-tip, a white wave wildly tumbling at him across the frozen surface of the loch where waves are stillborn, the crash of ice, the eerie lighting of a black loch backlit by the city, the weirdly lit grey-white of the swans' terrifying advance, the more terrifying for its elegance . . . the fox weighed it all up in a moment, and fled.

All I ever saw of it was the sudden galvanising of the un-bird-like shape, the unfurling of two ghosts. By the time I had fathomed the source of the disturbance and reconstructed the moment, the fox was beyond the furthest duck, a frantic retreating shadow among a mountain of shadows, retreating fast uphill. The swans slithered and subsided down on to the ice, cartwheeling ducks in every direction. Loud squadrons of them sprang into the night air and whirled across the mountain slope, fifty feet above the ice, crazy in the crowded sound and unclear sight of it all, but all of them alive to fly thanks to the vigilance and the supreme bullying overlordship of swans.

We retired, the fox and I, to such food and shelter as we would glean from the night city, and from our own very different points of view, to dwell on the ways of the white sentries of the winter night under an urban mountain. I wondered for the first time whether lesser wildfowl actually seek out the company of swans because it is safer to have them nearby, and the temperamental tyranny to which swans sometimes subject them is a small price to pay.

3

The Perfect Nest

HERE THEY COME AGAIN, a ragged fly-past of angels, dowdy and chaotic, thrashing every corner of the pond into a ferment, irresistible as a snow-plough, littering the banks and shallows with spoil heaps of demented coots and mallards and moorhens and all the other also-rans of the wildfowl kingdom which happen to get in the way. When a phalanx of mute swans takes flying lessons, the best course of action for these lesser fowl is to go somewhere else.

At nine abreast, and with the tutoring parents in front, the exertions of their dummy runs consume all the pond there is, which is roughly 250 yards by a hundred, and all the morning. Between sorties, the rest of the pond's teeming birdlife ventures tentatively back out on to the water to feed, squabble, flicker and sprint and saunter. Then the water at the far end erupts and all swannish hell breaks loose again, wings and black webs in tumult. If the fox of St Margaret's Loch had seen this scale of a wave unfurl towards him, he would have given up wildfowl for life and become vegetarian.

But this is West Lothian, a fat-of-the-land farmyard pond a dozen miles west of Edinburgh, where the spectral shapes of gaunt old pit bings (headstones to the long-dead shale-mining industry) suddenly relent to reveal a subtle green land beyond, a place of well-worked farms, a scatter of volcanic crags, a well-wooded place of subtle landscape charm and surprising wildlife riches. At its heart lies the swan pond, a small oasis of astounding swan fertility in an area of Scotland where in the recent past they have fared badly and now fare worse. For a few spring-into-summer months some years ago I pitched my relentless restlessness nearby and found many of life's difficulties assuaged by almost daily visits to the pond. It was then and there that swans ceased to be an interest and became a passion.

This pond is the perfect habitat for mute swans. I use the word advisedly. Nature does not design perfect habitats. This one has been designed by man, and long after the pond ceased to have a practical function as the power source for a threshing mill, and long after swans had first taken to its shores, its landscape was subtly re-shaped, its be-all-and-end-all became the welfare of swans, and under a conspiracy of benevolent forces, the swans have prospered.

Of course there are never just swans on such a delectable and comparatively safe haven of a watersheet. Watching the pond also provided a crash course in the behaviour patterns of commoner wildfowl of that land – mallard, tufted duck, teal, pochard, moorhens, coots, little grebes primarily – and sundry other small birds which strafe the water's droning insect hordes (finches, flycatchers, warblers swallows, swifts and martins), and a few of those bird tribes which make a living by making life a misery for the small birds (sparrow-hawks, magpies, the big gulls). Foxes inevitably home on the dusk-to-dawn pond to catch the nesting season's unwary, and in West Lothian you are never far from a badger sett, for these are the most densely populated badger miles in Scotland.

One of the benevolent forces is a well-disposed human population, the folk who live around the pond and along a mile of the farm track which skirts it. The first evening I ever spent here was memorable for an encounter with one of the natives, a farm worker with no ornithological inclination save for an instinctive Burns-like thirling to anything and everything which nature ever invented. The conversation began with a grunted greeting. I nodded at the swans on their island nest.

'Do they do well here?'

There was a long blank silence and a blank stare, during which I wondered if he was deaf. Then suddenly he said:

'Dae whit well?'

'I mean are they disturbed much?'

'Disturbed? Whae'd disturb swans? An' whit fur?'

'Lots of people do, though admittedly for no good reason. Fishermen for instance, sometimes.' I added the 'sometimes' cagily, in case I was treading on an angler's toes. I wasn't.

'Fishermen?' He spat. 'Na, there's nae fushin here. Nae fush. Ah'm catchin yur drift, sur. Na there's nae fushin' an there's nae ither buggar fushes for swans. We a' see to that. Aye, ah suppose yid say they dae well enough.'

'How many young? Last year, say?'

'Seven. Every year.'

'*Every* year?'

'Aye.'

'And how many usually make it to flying?'

'A've tellt ye. Seven.'

Incredulity and exasperation were setting in. His simplistic arithmetical confidence was unshakably based on ritual observation, day after day, 'fur mair nor twenty years, sur'. Because this was where he watched his swans, he had assumed that eggs equals chicks equals fledglings, matters of ritual unswayed by alien intervention. I tried to argue otherwise with him, citing fishing, pollution, lead poisoning, vandalism, disturbance, but he would have none of it. He turned to the pond and demanded my evidence which proved him wrong, and of course there was none, except that three days later she hatched eight. In the ten years from that date they hatched eight, eight, eight, eight, eight, eight, none (the cob disappeared in early spring, presumably having flown into overhead cables), nine, nine, nine, and fledged them all but one which was born with a genetic wing deformity. The average number of fledged birds from a single clutch is about three.

So eight more gather beyond my feet on a late September afternoon of coot-scratched glass calm, jostling in the degrees of their boldness for accustomed scraps, the adult birds stand-offish and wary, but just as eager to exert their pecking order priority if the pickings prove rich. Already the young birds have established different personalities, stamped them on my watching hours. There is one, identifiable for the moment by a whitened eye stripe, which is first to feed. His blunt head-on confrontationist approach leaves brothers and sisters in his wake. Another is faster, nimbler in pursuit of scattered morsels, avoids the bickering, the only one of the family to square up to the bold one and call his brazen bluff. Another lags furthest out, feeds least from the hand, and up-ends more than any of the others. She will fly the wildest of the brood.

The cob, unhungry, has distanced himself a little from the brood, thrown wide his wings, risen out of the water on his tail, and with neck straight and head tall, unleashed the widest scope of his wings, flayed the air three times. It is a gesture common to more or less all wildfowl, but only in swans is it a thing of power, grace, spectacle, theatre. In ducks it is a comic clockwork whir, in geese it is Pickwickian, preposterous. In swans, I am certain that whatever its value to the maintenance of plumage, it is also done for effect. I do not believe the bird is unaware of the impact of the gesture; it is indisputable overlordship, and pity the bird or beast which misreads it.

The wild one of the brood, now almost as far out from the bank as the cob, suddenly emulates the gesture (with none of the panache and only a suppressed hint of the power), and just as suddenly, the others are lured into a wide fanning formation strewn across the width of the pond. The start is ragged, like a Grand National and just as chaotic, but instantly galvanises noisily into its stride. The spectacle depends for effect as much on sound as sight. The sound is all of energy being expended, uncoordinated as yet but supercharged with potential – the slap of five-inch black webs as they kick back the pond's surface, devouring yards, the unique four-in-the-bar song of mute swan wings. That wingsong in a solo swan is such an elemental and familiar companion to the swan watcher. (The word 'swan' means 'sounder', almost certainly because the bird sounds with every wingbeat. Mute swan makes very little sense in any language.) To hear it eightfold in this ragamuffin concerto is to hear a favourite theme thrillingly if uncertainly re-orchestrated.

Dabchicks shriek in the path of the bird-wave as it breaks. Coots retreat, quibbling. Moorhens stand on the water and run offstage, blue-black on yellow stilts. Two young tufties stranded hopelessly far from cover eye the swans' advance and dive. The wave passes over, they resurface into the turbulence of its wake. You can almost sense the exchange: 'What the . . .?'

The water and the airspace, so often a farmyard cliché for tranquility where you fancy a Constable might have lingered, are suddenly a theatre for frenzy, but as the swans run out of steam and water and nerve, one shape, the wild swan of the brood, detaches from the crowd. She has space beneath her feet! She flies.

She clears the hawthorns by a foot and suddenly hers is the only wingbeat, she the only sounder. She flies for perhaps a minute, two rough circuits of the pond, a first glimpse of the wide world beyond its fringing trees. The shallow climb above farm buildings scatters a wire-ful of perched young swallows, queueing for Africa. They have seen nothing bigger than a crow in the air until now. What must they make of the sight and the sound of a passing swan ten feet away?

By the end of the afternoon, two more have flown, but the wild one's flight was the ice-breaker, and I suspect she can be as wild or as tame a swan as she wishes. She may well need to be both. She is, I am sure, a survivor.

I mark the significance of the day for this swan tribe I have watched since the end of the winter by staying on through the afternoon into the quickening September evening. I watched the pen lead her young back to the nest on its tiny island, the nest itself now a bedraggled and barely recognisable parody of its vast nursery snugness, but still a symbol of some security. They follow her as they have always followed her, disciplined and obedient. As they climb from the water, a small panic of bloody-nosed young moorhens speeds away from the island like pellets from a scattergun, to be herded into a controllable mass by their parents, and once the swans are ensconced, led back to the deepest shadow of the island rocks where their own half-hearted nest was thrown together.

The cob stays out late on the water, ink-black now against the pale-fired sunset pond like a negative of a swan. There is the air of a leisured and regal procession about his small kingdom, for ducks defer, coots part or chitter discreetly from the reeds. The swallows skim across his bows, pillaging amid the insect towers which stand above the water, an elegant slaughter. The cob sails at last to my trackside, and with the last of the pink light on him, stands flamingo-tall to preen.

It is at this point that many nature-watchers are consumed by roosting notions of their own, and slip with the sun below their own horizons, but I have long since learned to love the hour of the half-light of any season, shivering cheerfully enough in the gathering folds of the night cloak. Besides, gloamings of early September are hardly a penance of discomfort. I have rarely managed to summon the dedication of the dawn riser (my dawn watches are usually the last snatches of all-through-the-night watches), but the slow dusk-into-dark shifts of the landscape contours suit my frame of mind and are the justification of this philosophy. The dawn watcher has no logical sense of a vigil completed; his tranquillities inevitably fail him as the morning grows, the mortal world awakes, the dawn magic rubs off, and whatever the joy of his dawn hour, he is faced with anti-climax. The dusk watcher's day winds down with his roosting charges, and the furtive unveiling of night lives is a lower profile of nature which harmonises with his mood. He retires replete because he has worked with the grain of the wilds, not against it. He marks the hours with the chimes of roosting pheasants, the squeaking-frog patrols of roding woodcock, the passing of the laws of daylight with shuttered suns, the dawn of the moon regime with the back-and-forth echo of tawny owls across the wood, the three-syllable shout of the vixen, the mobilising of moles. It is good because it fits.

So now on the swan pond it is the owl hour. These are well-wooded acres, the county as rich in badgers as it once was in mine-workings. From the tall pond-fringing beeches, a wheezy young tawny owl splutters a thin unpractised asthmatic hoot, untranquil on the evening air if you like your owl vowels rounded, but music to my pondside ears because it is of its time of day and season of the year, and in its place. The adult reassurance from a distant pine sparks off a sweet-and-sour conversation which will last an hour.

Meanwhile there are liberty-takers afloat, relishing the sudden swanlessness. With the mutes safe on the island there is conspicuously more room for lesser pond-dwellers, and the shyest of these take their ease now in streaming single file from the furthest reeds – a family of little grebes, or dabchicks, or dive-dapper, or dive-dop, or dooker, or mither-of-the-mawkins, or tom-puddin, or penny-bird, or drink-a-penny, and doubtless any number of other dialectic variations which I have not stumbled across. (Beware of rival dialects which call moor-hens dabchicks as well. The linguistics of nature can be a confusing science.) The soprano horse-laugh of the adults is a favourite song of the pond, and once you learn to associate it with that unlikeliest of sources (it would sound much better coming from a magpie, or a green woodpecker), you begin to realise there is a well-concealed charisma about the little grebe, dabchick, and the rest.

What looks like a misshapen piece of floating builders' rubble when you see it from ahead or astern and in silhouette becomes a darkly

44

exotic little creature, ten inches from stem to stern, chestnut-throated and cheeked, black-skulled, brown-backed, and given to throwing up a miniature white fan on its rump. It also has a neat trick of submerging itself when danger threatens, all but its head and the top half of its neck which watches like a very short periscope. It heaps an apology of a nest on the surface of the water, a thing of weeds and scum and muck and mud, anchored by willpower, and floating despite itself. It passes winter away in grey-white anonymity, and somewhere else, for its goonish giggle is utterly absent from the pond, and only returns just before the martins in early spring. A discreet and intriguing bird, until its opens it mouth.

At this hour, however, they are respectfully quiet, feeding by diving for sticklebacks or snapping for insects. Even the coots are reduced to muted bickerings, chipping away doggedly at anything which threatens to sound like a protracted silence.

If anything out-populates the coots hereabouts it is the mallards, and these gather in new-found bravado around the island's base and – in a clear gesture of collective provocation – about the feet of the preening cob. Even I, a mere unwebbed non-wildfowl, can see the gesture's folly. I can only guess at how a standing swan seems through mallard eyes from somewhere about ankle height, but I would guess it is daunting enough. When the swan then spreads a furlong of wings with the apparent intention of using mallards as stepping-stones there would seem to be some merit in retreat to reconsider the folly of the escapade from afar. Mallards scatter in every direction but mine, mine being landlocked, while the cob makes a token neck-lowered dash at the nearest retreating tail. The mallards swim off under full sail to the safe gloom of the far shore, where they reassemble in good order, standing one-footed to preen, the incident already obliterated, I fancy, from memory.

The swan's return to the water drives the grebes back into their reedy seclusion, but undaunted coots and moorhens still stream across the pond on small jerky missions. On the island, the pen and her eight young have draped necks far down spines, their heads pillowed deep in the most sumptuous of feather-bedding. The cob kills thirty minutes patrolling the dusky water, a monarch putting the lieges in their proper, lesser place, then retires himself to the island. The water stills, grows darker, quieter, the owls grow louder, and senses become preoccupied with small rustlings in hedge and bush and undergrowth. There is nothing to focus on now, so I watch the sky for passing silhouettes, and turn an ear on the pond and away from a new night wind. A far commotion of mallard and coot and tufted duck and others unidentifiable in the sudden startling throng of noise may – or may not – mark the presence of one of the neighbourhood foxes, but from this distance, in this light, there is no telling. Perhaps the dawn-riser will find a pool of feathers, a stain of small slaughter, in which case, he will be one up on me.

Two months from now the swans will have gone, the little grebes will have gone, so too the martins, swifts, swallows, most of the tufted duck, many of the coots and moorhens, to be replaced by a handful of winter fly-by-nights, pochard, wigeon perhaps. It is a lot to lose. But every winter is thick with memories of the wild year that has just ebbed out of reach.

4
The Flaw

THE JACKDAWS would be the first to know. There were nineteen in the tops of the highest pondside beeches one grey ice-cold midwinter day. From there they could see far over the pale, comatose landscape of that season. Their naturally keen sight would detect movement low over that rise in the ground which obscures the firth. Not geese. The light caught that movement in a way which it does not catch the geese. It was a different enough movement to catch and hold the jackdaws' attention, white movement against the lowest quarter of the grey northern sky. They saw great wingbeats, oddly irregular at first until, as the fliers came on, they could differentiate two sets of wings, one swan so close behind and above the other that their wings seemed to intertwine in the confusing perspective of that distance. Soon the sound of the wings was on the jackdaws' ears, and the unwavering beeline of swanflight making straight for them identified the birds to the jackdaws. The pond swans were returning. It was January 25 and they had been gone two months.

I did not see them arrive, although I had lingered expectantly around the pond two days earlier. What I saw then was a solid sheet of ice I could walk on, a milling of uncountable mallards in the furthest corner where the pack bustled to keep open water about them. In the tallest beeches were nineteen jackdaws. I heard, but did not see a coot. A heron came and furled his winter-weary cloak but did not linger. There was precious little scope for him in what was left of the pond. What was not frozen was mallard.

There was a snell and subtle hint of a north-westerly tipping the balance of the swans' journey as they flew down the in-by fields, a

snow-wind, tangy as woodsmoke. The birds would circle the pond
sun-wise and turn into that wind to land. They would put down in
the nearest half of the pond and hit the ice too hard, for they had
grown unaccustomed to it: two unfreezing winters in a row and they
had not had to negotiate an ice landing for three years. They controlled
their slowing two-footed slide well enough though, and crossed on
foot to the ducks, which would regard them as a mixed blessing. They
might resent the instant dominance (but defer to it), and relish the
security and strength the swans represent. The strength was put to
work at once, and within hours they had beaten the ice back another
few precious yards, and for the rest of that freezing week, the swans
towered over the press of mallards, and the ice was beaten back and
back, inches at a time, and the open water sanctuary at the corner of
the pond grew imperceptibly, and was safe. It was good to have them
again, the mallard and I agreed.

I saw them first on January 31. The bird count that afternoon was
two mute swans, one moorhen, ninety-four mallards, and there was
water enough for a lingering but unrewarded visit from the heron.
But there would be much about the return of the swans which only
the jackdaws know.

There were other eyes watching for the return of the swans,
watching from a pondside cottage called 'Mallards'. I have already
described the pond as the perfect mute swan habitat, and it is perfect
because Brian and Barbara Cadzow made it that way, and maintain it
that way. Brian Cadzow grew up in the big old farmhouse which
dominates the heart of the farm and throws a winter shadow far across
the pond. 'I had my tonsils out on the kitchen table,' he recalls, but
the memory is a more affectionate tribute to the house as childhood
home than medical grimace. There are two other houses around the
pond, well spaced, and both architecturally rooted unmistakably in
the last third of the twentieth century. One is called 'The Swannery',
the other 'Mallards'. The Cadzows built them both, and lived in them
in turn, moving sun-wise round the pond as they grew older and their
needs dwindled. Mallards, their small retirement house, is designed
and sited as much to accommodate the well-being of the swans as the
two people who live there. For all that Brian has had an adventurous
globe-trotting life as farmer and government adviser and much else
besides, the farm has been the root from which life has branched for

all his seventy-three years. So there is an attachment, a thing of belonging, to this land that is so often at the heart of thoughtful land management wherever you encounter it. He can give you a detailed potted history of the place without recourse to a single reference document.

The farm was built in 1823, the pond created seven years later to serve a threshing mill. The housing for the mill wheel is still there, a forty-foot-deep abyss in a farm shed, the whole thing fashioned and lined with stone, a gloomily impressive monument to the mason's art. Brian Cadzow's father took over the tenancy of the farm in 1905, Brian himself bought it in 1950, and having now retired, his son runs it. It is managed today with all the efficiency of the era, but through the simple fact of the ninety years of the Cadzow regime, there is a clear respect for what it has been, and the hint of regret at what agriculture has become is unconcealed. Brian quotes some turn-of-the-century facts of farm life:

'There was a man's grieve and a woman's grieve, and between them they had more than a hundred people working under them.'

But doing what?

'Well, for example, all the fields had hedges, and every hedge was cut twice a year, and dug twice a year to keep it free of weeds.' Now, well, spot the hedge . . . and the whole farm is run with a staff of two.

There is also another legacy of that far-off era, another unbroken thread as long as the twentieth century, and possibly longer – the mute swans on the pond. All Brian can say with any certainty is that 'they've been here as long as I have', but there is no reason to doubt that the pond has hosted swans for almost as long as it has been a pond.

A closer involvement with the swans began in 1960 when a conservatory was built behind the old farmhouse. For the first time the Cadzows had a window with an unobscured view of the water. A little ingenuity and a lot of labour lured the swans centre-stage. The traditional nest site was on the west bank of the pond where it suffered too much disturbance for the swans' comfort; eggs were lost and the persistent attentions of young boys in particular badly affected the birds' breeding success. Improvised deterrents included the back of an old car arranged round the landward side of the nest by a farm worker, which may have won a respite for the swans, but hardly assisted the cause of the local landscape.

The lasting solution was an island. It gave sanctuary for the swans, and by siting it opposite the conservatory, an endless source of wonder and delight for pondside humans. The following winter's deep freeze made for the perfect island-building conditions. Rocks were sledged across the ice, dropped into holes, built up above the surface, rubble and soil were heaped inside the stone circle, a weeping willow was planted to shade a sitting swan, and – the final temptation to lure the pair away from the bank – a bale of straw was left on the new island. Mute swans have never been the shrewdest of nesters, and the sites chosen by some pairs are just downright baffling, but the pond pair recognised the merits of the island at once, and moved straight in.

Year by year, their fledging performance improved. The old site yielded broods of threes and fours, but on the island it was soon up to six, then a long run of sevens 'fur mair nor twenty years', give or take the lapse in concentration of a year or two on the part of my first pondside informant. (Somewhere along the line, that long run of sevens may well have produced the seventh swan of a seventh swan, which considering how nature has bestowed her favours on the tribe of swans, should be quite a bird.) Then there were a few years of eights, a blank year in the mid-eighties when the cob disappeared in the spring, presumably a casualty of pylon wires which claim the lives of so many swans, but then three nines, and the Cadzows on the edge of their seats with the address of the Guinness Book of Records in hand in case she produced four nines in a row.

Sitting in the Cadzows' small lounge with the Peter Scott paintings on the wall, you can watch real-life Scotts coursing past the floor-to-ceiling window every few minutes for it is a window on the world of the pond which is never still and never devoid of swan or wildfowl. Here I have listened to Brian's swan-husbandry philosophies with a mixture of envy and admiration.

For twenty years now, the Cadzows have managed their pond strictly as a nature reserve, the prime purpose of which is to champion the swans' cause. There is no fishing (except for the little grebes, the heron, the occasional passing cormorant), no shooting (a silly exercise hereabouts in any case, when you can take out a dozen mallards by hitting them over the head as they pass), no concessions to the pleasures of people other than that simplest age-old pleasure of watching wildlife at close quarters, the pleasure compounded by the theatre of swans.

'So how,' Brian Cadzow was saying, 'do you get nine young three years in a row, and all the rest? Well, if you want a lot of lambs you make sure the ewes are well fed. Same with swans. We see to it that they're well fed.'

So every morning a farmhand has the extra duty, surely unique on a modern farm, of laying out a sack of oats for the swans, and whenever silos are being cleaned out, the surplus grain also goes to the swans. The pond's three households also see to it that the supply is topped up with bread and other morsels, and few visitors who come to see the cygnets come empty handed.

'That, and lack of disturbance – very important for mute swans. That's the secret.'

That and the determined effort to achieve the perfect habitat, the sustained commitment of more than thirty years' hard labour which is their way of returning nature's compliment. Nature provides the swans from which they have derived so much pleasure. They assist nature in the most practical way, and between them, they are responsible for giving something like 220 mute swans the perfect start in life.

Occasionally, a little manipulation of the landscape has been necessary over the years. A large hawthorn tree used to stand at the west end of the pond, and because the young swans insist on flying practice en masse, it was invariably on the flightpath of one of them, and getting airborne has always been difficult enough for a young swan without a flightpath littered with immovable objects. The memory of it convulses their benefactor.

'They used to land right in the top of the bloody thing. It looks so undignified, a swan up a tree.'

The tree had to go.

Stories flow through the afternoon while out on the pond the cob preens and the pen dozes on the island and beneath her one more brood begins the transition from a speck of life-dust to one of nature's supreme creations. While the miracle unfolds, all our conjecturing is about how many miracles she's sitting on. Nine more? Double figures for the first time?

The talk turns to the cob.

'Saw him kill another swan once. Another cob landed on the pond and he just went for him. I saw the fight, couldn't intervene. There was no boat handy – it was over at the farm. By the time I got back with it the intruder was dead on the bank'.

The clipped, almost shorthand stacatto of the account was too fast, too perfunctory. I wanted to slow him down. I wanted the blow by blow account, the preliminaries, the contest, the denouement, but another story was already rippling on the surface of memory, to be told while it surfaced, before it dived down again into the unordered depths of what must be a vast store.

'There was a time we blacked out half of West Lothian. The cob had driven off an intruder and it flew off straight into some high-tension wires. It was like a bomb going off. I had roast swan in my hands, but it knocked out the electricity supply across the north of the county. I phoned the board, but they said they couldn't restore power until they knew what the fault was. I said I had the fault in my hands. It was a swan. But they would do nothing until they came out to see the thing for themselves.'

Then there was the year the resident swans got hungry.

'For some reason they must have felt there wasn't enough food here. The chicks were just a few weeks old. First I knew was a phone call from the farm three-quarters of a mile away. "Brian, I've got your swans here. I think they're hungry. What do I do about it?" They had *walked* three quarters of a mile, including crossing the main road, to another source of food, then when they'd been fed, they walked back. Now how did the swans know to do that?'

There are many documented cases of swans leading newly hatched cygnets on perilous journeys both on water and by land to suitable feeding waters (the adults having ignored the seemingly obvious requirement of good feeding for the young near the nest, and often repeating the journey from the same unsuitable nest site year after year), but this is the first one I have encountered where the journey was both the solution to a temporary problem – suggesting the adults had both recognised the problem and worked out a solution – and where the behaviour was an isolated incident.

The talk drifted to some of the other inhabitants of the pond. One of the Cadzows' nearest neighbours is a little grebe with a nest under a pondside tree. The Cadzows know her well.

'Stray too close and she slips off the nest, pulls some scum over the eggs – it's a pretty scummy sort of nest anyway – swims off underwater, then surfaces to watch you from a few yards out.'

She does, too, and I can almost sense the tiny dark staring eye assessing my presence, my threat, quiet and alert and confident in the half-lit realm of the overhanging pondside and its murky shallows. Retreat to a hidden vantage point and see her dive again, resurface where you least expect her, and slip back onto the flimsy security of the nest and sit. The dark eye, though, never rests. There is something swarthy about little grebes, a certain mystery about their off-season movements, and just enough of an exotic hint in their summer garb and their habits to suggest a gypsy-ish air. Not so much a nest as an untidy encampment, not so much a migrant as an itinerant vagrant. A character, and crafty and charismatic with it.

'You should see her with the swans,' said Brian Cadzow. 'If they come too close to the nest she slips off, comes up behind them underwater, nips the tail of the nearest bird, dives again, and swims off ten yards then surfaces to watch the reaction.'

The reaction is usually an irritated hiss, but there is little the swan can do about it. The hissing bit is a long way from the tail tweaker and manoeuvrability is not one of the bird's gifts. The little grebe, by contrast, employs quicksilver guile as a way of life. The swans pose no real threat to her but the sheer size of the birds too near her nest must be an unnerving presence, such as a featherweight inadvertently cornered by a heavyweight might feel, even though they won't be in the same bout. So the little grebe uses her best defence in an almost mischievous manner, knowing that from behind the swan is an easy target without fear of serious retribution. In that, she has something in common with crows, of all things. Keith Brockie has two nicely observed sketches in his *Wildlife Sketchbook* of a crow venturing a similar assault on a Bewick swan which was grazing in a stubble field. He noted:

Whilst sketching I was intrigued to watch a carrion crow striding up to a pair of Bewicks. To my astonishment it proceeded to pull the swan's tail, only jumping back when the swan lashed out angrily at it. This 'cat-and-mouse' game went on for fully five minutes, the swan even had to put up with another crow which joined in for a few pulls. I can think of no other reason for this behaviour than sheer devilment.

Crows are masters of mischief-making of course, and there is a sense of the same devil-may-care in little grebes, although it is nothing less than in character that the bird should turn its mischievous streak to practical ends. On the West Lothian pond, it works, and one pull is usually enough to deflect the trespassing swan in search of its invisible antagonist.

'What else?' Brian Cadzow interrogated himself. 'Mallards of course, everywhere. They even nest up trees, and one nested on top of a ten-feet-high garden wall. She has to get the young quickly to the pond because they must feed themselves right from the start. She just kicks them off the wall. They survive.'

The idea of day-old mallards being nudged (that 'kicked' was a little poetic licence, although it does conjure up a good cartoonish image) by their mother into the bewilderment of thin air and the brief freefall down the cliff face of the wall is one of nature's black-comedy gestures. She has a sense of the absurd, mother nature. I caught myself thinking of that scene from *The Magnificent Seven* in which Steve McQueen tells the story of the man who jumped off a tall building. As he fell, the people on each floor heard him assess his own progress . . . 'So far, so good . . . so far, so good . . .' Usually the mallard chicks land intact. Then their troubles really begin, for not even as carefully controlled a pro-duck environment as this can spare a new mallard brood from the ravages of predators. They are simply easy meat, and work on the principle of safety in numbers, but all that is safe is the survival of the species. There are an awful lot of mallards here, but one-in-seven is a reasonable educated guess at the survival rate of individuals.

As we swopped mallard stories, a pair sped through the window's wide panorama of the pond, a low chase which landed loudly a dozen yards from the Cadzows' front door. There they began the more-or-less synchronised head-dipping ritual of their tribe's graceless court-ship. They looked briefly like bad puppets inexpertly operated. Then the chase erupted again and the birds disappeared beyond the window. It happens so often in the lounge of that house called 'Mallards' whenever the talk turns to wildfowl. You look out as you talk and find yourself confirmed or confounded by what is happening before your eyes.

I kept dragging my mind's eye back to the gladiatorial encounter of the two cobs which ended in the death of the interloper. I was impressed by that dark irony of nature. Here is a county where swans have suffered dire fortunes in recent years. At its heart is this small oasis of astounding fertility, so conspicuous to one restless, frustrated and eagerly mature swan that the most profound of dilemmas was confronted and resolved. Faced with a dearth of habitable territory, the pond is an irresistibly seductive opportunity worth the ultimate risk, worth dying for, and worth taking the life of another swan. Swans do not, it seems, adhere to the ancient belief, still held among the old folk of Celtic realms – Ireland and westmost Scotland in particular – that a swan should never be harmed because the bird might be host to the soul of a loved one. Swans are the guardian symbols of the human soul, but who knows or even cares about the destiny of a swan's soul? We have invested swans with our own symbolism. We surely cannot then look on a fight to the death as merely the law of the jungle, dismissable with that old 'nature can be cruel' cliché?

Later that day, on reading over notes based on our conversation, another aspect of the duel on the pond occurred to me which heightened my fascination for what I had already decided was a singular experience. The resident cob had as likely as not killed his own 'son'. It is certainly tempting to identify the vanquished challenger as a bird hatched and raised on the pond. It is such an isolated place in terms of swans (on no flightpath and with no scope for winter gatherings) and so many young birds have flown from its island sanctuary it is unthinkable that none of the pond's maturing offspring should try to resolve the problem of finding a territory by going home. The pond is also such a safe place that its security is surely imprinted on the mind of a swan which, in its wandering immature years, will have learned just how insecure the rest of that landscape is. So the perfection of the pond as swan habitat would be an even stronger pull.

Parental respect would not be a deterrent. The commonest way of breaking up a fully fledged swan family in any one year is that the cob drives out any lingering young, violently if necessary. It is likely that

the returning challenger three or four years later would recognise not
a father figure but only an obstacle to winning a great territorial prize.

So my mind had set the scene for a knightly encounter, the landscape
of the pond its own enclosed arena, the lesser fowl a nervous skulking
audience gawping from reed bed and woody shore:

> Unarmoured, he was his own
> lance and white charger,
> feared none but his own
> kind.
>
> Unshielded, he rode down
> the firth's wide and salty winds,
> speared the air alone
> and shunned
>
> unbonded flocks of swans.
> He was equipped with all
> swans' needs and also owned
> the soul
>
> unliberated of one
> whose life ebbed out
> from island childhood, song
> unsung,
>
> unheard by all save swans
> attuned to such
> a listless and lone one:
> its radiance
>
> undulled by age, shone
> childlight on swanflight's
> memory of a distant pond.
> There
>
> unarmoured, and fearing none
> but the swan he dared,
> died where he was born
> and dying

saw the child soul fly on
free as any bird but swan.

So those are the Cadzows and their pond, and the kind of talk and thoughts which spill out from their window-walled lounge when swans are on the agenda. Last year the swans all left at once, for the second consecutive year, a change in the pattern of the pond where in earlier years the cob has had to drive out his progeny. Now it was January 31, the day smothered in a half-dark steel-grey shawl by mid-afternoon, and I had driven the farmtrack to the pond anticipating the return of the swans. They were there, at the far corner of the pond, knee deep in mallards, and I acknowledged that, at the sight of them, winter felt a little less relentless.

The throng of birds milled energetically about their corner of open water, all bar an admiring ring of one-footed ice-perched mallard spectators. The ice was thick and unyielding, the sky wore the same deep grey as the ice, the reed beds were brittle and pale and colourless, the trees skeletally patient as herons, the landscape a glowering and unfathomable thing. But the swans were back, their presence a white heat to thwart the worst excesses of the ice and to rekindle in me the same old quiet anticipatory thrill at the prospects of the wild year ahead.

Two weeks later, the only thing which had changed was that winter had deepened, snow had fallen steadily and daily for ten days and between falls the temperature dropped and the cold bit. The birds were still gathered in the same corner, restlessly holding the ice at bay, and in more or less the same numbers.

There is a simple rule for watching the same wild creatures regularly and it is to ritualise your presence – the same approach, the same behaviour, the same clothing. That way, there is at least the chance that the wildlife you are watching will come to recognise you eventually and, if you have established the right kind of presence, single you out from other human traffic at least as a source of no threat. It is easier with some forms of wildlife and impossible with some others. It may sound a poor reward for a lot of painstaking effort, but it is all most of us are entitled to expect, and if you can achieve it, you can see and understand and learn much. The ones who can go beyond that, and elicit a positive response in wild creatures are a rare tribe, an endangered species themselves. My friend Mike Tomkies is one such. But sometimes the odd incident occurs to repay the pains taken, some isolated gesture which offers a glimpse into the realm of that more rarified tribe of wildlife watchers, as though through a half-open door. Such a gesture now unfolded, the more remarkable because I had a premonitory sense that it was about to happen moments before it did.

I had cut the car engine and coasted the last few unseen yards down the track, as I always do, and stopped as quietly as possible by the pond. (Most wildlife responds much less warily to a car than to its dismounted occupants, and in some circumstances it can make an ideal hide.) As I rolled down the window and put the glasses on that far crowded corner of the pond I sensed a galvanising reaction in the cob. An instant later, he galvanised, but I am quite clear in my own mind that that was the sequence of events, that no sooner had the expectant seed sown itself than the swan breasted the ice rim, stepped hugely on to the ice itself with wings wide, ran a few wide-winged steps, then flew. There was no hint of doubt that I was the object of his attention, just as there was no doubt that his purpose was anything other than benign. The swan was a low and unswerving arrow directed straight at me, and for all the familarities of the sight and sound and character of the flight, and for all that I sat in the unconducive cocoon of the car, the flight now dissolved into a figment of dream and I saw it with the exaggerated clarity of a slow-motion film. The swan had less than 200 yards to fly, its illusory aspect doubtless heightened by the confounding perspective of the glasses, but it came endlessly on, the progress of a timeless creation of nature graced by a raw beauty. It was thus for the first flight of the first swan of all.

In the ice, the bird's reflection was an abstracted blur, a thing of shade and rhythm rather than a definable inverted swan shape. The bird flew so low over the ice that the wings' downstroke brushed the surface several times, and the pulsing song of the wings bounced back from the ice so that the sound seemed to emanate from the contact of wingtip and ice and echo back into the long sculpted caves of the underwings. At last the rhythm faltered, the wings heaved high and held there while the bird reared in the air and pushed forward the biggest webbed feet in the wilds, dropped easily to a controlled ice landing, subsided into the slushy no-man's-land of my shore. Without pause, he stepped up the bank, crossed the few yards of grass bank and verge and stopped dead with his face two feet from mine. From there he regarded me with brilliant black eyes down the orange blaze of his beak. I spoke a few quiet words of greeting, but as I reached for a piece of bread, he turned, crossed back to the pond and walked leisurely back across the ice to the pen and the mallard throng. I had been recognised, met, and greeted, and I will not be convinced otherwise. No other bird stirred, and if it had been a feeding foray, why not stay to eat? The pen would certainly have come too. Perhaps it was all nothing more than that the consuming business of the day was at the other end of the pond, keeping open water in that corner where feeding is reliable and regular from the houses there. My presence was an excuse for the swan to fulfil his need to express *his* presence on *his* territory, and having fulfilled that need, he simply returned to the job in hand.

I left the place in a state of mild elation, the friend of swans!

The encounter haunted me for days. It was made the more powerful by the familiarity of the surroundings, and I believe it is that specific coincidence of the fey and the familiar which is at the heart of man's mythical and artistic relationship with swans; it is hardly unlikely that something should rub off when a writer with some of the instincts of a nature-poet goes wandering among swans. With the cob, the moment would be over in the instant. With me it will never be over. I will see for ever that bright swan detach itself from the humdrum dullness of a winter's day and burn its flight into my mind with all the clarity of a Bewick engraving, a Tunnicliffe painting.

Was it such a flight which spoke directly to a Nordic bard centuries ago? Did he so ache for a reciprocal response in the swan that he wrote the encounter as he wished it had been, and so established the idea of the interchangeability of man and swan, setting down the first swan myth?

It was the end of February before the ice relented. I returned on a day of soft rain, the snow reduced to long drab streaks on the high ground, or wedged grubbily under the lee of an old hedge. The pond was busier by far. Several mallards were displaying in that deranged clockwork style they have, moorhens stuttered across the pond and skulked the shore, a few tufted ducks were back and half a dozen wintering pochard hadn't left yet. The little grebes still hadn't returned from their wintering wherevers. I watched the swans for two hours during which they swam companionably close, circled the nest island twice anti-clockwise, came ashore to ask for food – a soft two-syllable contralto grunt from each bird – and to preen.

Only the cob will take food from my hand, his beak as hard and ragged-edged as a razor shell. The pen stays out of arm's reach, making an intimidating hiss with beak open and long tongue prominent if I move too quickly. Then they both retire a few yards to preen. Their plumage is in peak condition, a vivid brightness geared to the seductions of the breeding season which, for this pair at least, is about to begin.

Far to the northwest I have begun to watch a second pair whose fortunes on the wild edge of a highland loch will contrast markedly with this pair in their safe haven. The Highlanders' story comes later, but now, as the pond pair contemplate putting their house in order on a custom-built site, their Highland kin are contemplating new blizzards on that mountain which shutters the sun from the loch for three-quarters of the winter. Before they find a serviceable nest site, they will have to thole not just the blizzards, not just the ice, but also the annual havoc-wreaker in that land, the floods. It will be a long, long haul.

Here on the pond, winter is done. I watch the two swans preen and wonder how aware they are of the privilege they enjoy. Both will have been through the trying years of immaturity, the quest for territory, but do they bless the fates which lured them to this small swan paradise, or do they register none of that, accept the good hand fate dealt them and respond to it by taking all its advantages to produce as many swans as that benevolence will allow? The pen is preening the inside of one wing, making it buffet like a sail. The cob, too, is working down one wing, but a feather masks one eye giving him an absurdly coy look. It is a good thing to do, to sit within touching distance of a pair of mature mute swans at the beginning of their new life-cycle, to be a small part of the continuity of that life-cycle having watched it unfold, off and on, over a decade. It is by going over the same ground, scrutinising the same rituals and set pieces of nature, comparing and contrasting the year ahead with the

Early summer and the pond family take their ease
Even at a few days old cygnets flex their 'wings'

Bathing sequence . . . A bathing swan preens vigorously, rolls on to its back almost submerged and thrashes the water with its wings

Attentive pen keeps watch over her brood

Cygnet's eye-view of its father

one before and the one before that . . . It is by that method and that method alone that you begin to come close to nature, begin to achieve a rapport of a kind (however frail and flawed) with wildness and wild creatures. There is no short cut.

I once interviewed the late David Stephen, one of Scotland's greatest naturalists, then aged seventy-four, and asked him what ambitions he still cherished in terms of wildlife. 'I want to know more about it, son,' he said. For that you need the patience (if not the other virtues) of a saint, and you need a compulsive and tireless fascination for your subject. So it is with me and swans.

Early March, and they swim close, head and neck tall, facing each other, and with neck feathers standing out like a fine fur, they begin to turn their heads from side to side. The display lasts perhaps twenty seconds, then they turn and swim on. It is a prelude to the complexities of the mating ceremony, a commitment, I believe, between the birds. Swans are more or less monogamous, and pair for life, and I am sure that this simple initial gesture binds them to another season together. The nest is almost ready, the dregs of last season's edifice have been smothered and embellished by the Cadzows' thoughtful annual bale of straw. It is perhaps six feet wide, and she has fashioned a pronounced cup in the top for the eggs. Out on the pond they pause again for more head-turning. It is a calm, pretty gesture.

Through March the pace of pond life begins to quicken. The little grebes are mysteriously back, and at once their giggling call seems to add a new and more determined layer of spring to the place. The mallard population thickens and there are sporadic mating frenzies in every corner of the pond, so many that you begin to realise why they have taken to the walls and trees to nest. There are simply not enough reeds to go round. The tufted ducks are discreet by comparison, a clannish lot, keeping to the reediest end of the pond, diving neatly to feed, a quiet and unfussy tribe, which in the context of the spring and summer pond, makes them unique.

The coots, for example, are ill-natured, foul-mouthed little presbyterian demons which abhor stillness as determinedly as nature does her vacuum. Fights are ten a penny, sometimes fatal. There are at least half a dozen breeding pairs on the pond, each of them responsible for two or three broods anything up to eight at a time. A coot at ease is either dead or asleep.

Moorhens share many of these characteristics, but they have the merit of bringing colour to the scene. Nature's colour chart has been lavished on this bird with no great thought for colour coding – yellow-tipped scarlet bill, dark orange eye, blue-black plumage with white wing and tail flashes, and the same bizarre colouring on the legs that distinguishes the bill, this time with the proportions reversed – scarlet 'garters', yellow shanks. A moorhen in full sunlight is a giddy sight.

These then are the swans' bedfellows as they approach the crux of the wild year. As March waxes more and more springlike the swans begin their mating ritual, a wild theatre of extravagant gesture and grace. It begins apparently haphazardly enough, the pair swimming close together and seemingly feeding with their heads underwater. A subtle evolution of the gesture begins until after several minutes both birds are dipping their heads underwater then raising them clear of the water in perfect unison. The impression is that they are bowing to each other. Then breast-to-breast they rise from the water and entwine necks, and there is no more eloquent single movement in all the expressionful repertoire of a swan's neck than this, no more eloquent single movement in all nature. She turns from him, then he mounts her back, takes the nape of her neck in his bill, and gives a convincing performance of trying to drown her. Her head stays under for so long that it is impossible not to become alarmed for her life, no matter how often you have seen swans mate. Yet she always surfaces unscathed if undignified. Then breast-to-breast again, they rise high on the water, and shout their exultant snorting approval of the moment. After that they preen and bathe heartily, and the supremely contained elegance of the ritual disintegrates explosively. The water around them seethes in the abandon of aftermath. Indeed you can be forgiven for thinking that you have just borne witness to the perfect consummation of nature, such is the sustained and poetic impact of the whole ritual from beginning to end.

Mike Birkhead and Christopher Perrins write in *The Mute Swan*: 'Mating and courtship displays take place mostly prior to egg-laying but they are not exclusive to this time of year and occur far more frequently than is required to fertilise the clutch. They may be an important factor in maintaining the pair bond.' Put like that, it sounds so like a marriage guidance counsellor emphasising the value of a good sex life to a healthy marriage that you are confronted again with all the swannish overtones which man has wished on himself, everything from *Swan Lake* to the guardianship of our souls to poet Tessa Ransford's almost casual PS: 'It is almost like a human being in flight.' It is a dull and unthinking soul – certainly not one in the keeping of swans – who watches the spring rites of mute swans and sees only two birds protecting the future of the species.

She has begun to lay by March 20, and a long and arduous process begins. A swan egg is huge – almost five inches long and three wide – so laying is hardly like shelling peas. She will lay one every two days, so if she is running true to form on the pond, the clutch will take more than two weeks to complete. Between eggs, she feeds with noticeable determination, for when she finally settles to incubate, she will be there for thirty-five days, during which she may not feed at all, and she may lose as much as a third of her body weight. The way to insure against that is to get heavy. During the laying days, the cob is often dutifully protecting the eggs while she feeds, keeping them warm and safe, but such is the ideal nature of the pond's nest site that he needs to be much less dutiful than many a cob. The site has other attributes too which legislate in favour of nature. Birkhead and Perrins write:

> We do not know what actually triggers egg-laying in swans. In most bird species, the individuals become more sexually active as the days lengthen in spring. The actual date on which mute swans start laying however, varies in relation to a number of factors. One of these is winter temperature: the warmer the months of December, January and February, the earlier the swans start laying. This link with winter temperature almost certainly arises because temperature affects plant growth (the food supply), which in turn affects clutch-size and breeding success.

The Cadzows' careful management of the pond, the sheltered nature of the pond itself, and immunity from dependence on plant growth as a food supply, are all factors which neutralise the effects of winter. After two consecutive and dramatically different winters, the swans would begin to hatch this year within two days of last year's date. So every conceivable advantage is at their disposal. They can nest early and lay early every year, and it is proved that the earlier the clutch is layed, the bigger it will be, and the better the chances of fledging success.

'Over-the-top conservationists,' protests Brian Cadzow, 'are the bane of my life.' Yet in the eyes of most naturalists, his is an extraordinary devotion to conservation of the most practical kind, the kind that gives nature a shot in the arm and ensures that the dosage is always available when it is needed. What has turned him against conservationists as a species is the heavy handed born-to-rule officiousness which often permeates organised conservation's worst excesses, and which he has met head-on more than once. One such occasion was a request from a body (which had better remain anonymous) to ring a particular brood. Brian consented, and the ringers duly arrived with a vanful of equipment including canoes, dinghies, and wetsuits.

Once it was made clear that the intention was to launch the boats on the pond, round up the cygnets, keep the adults at bay and generally cause mayhem among the wildfowl, Brian made it equally clear that they would do no such thing. He relieved them of the rings, fitted them alone and without fuss, and sent the chastened do-gooders packing.

Such encounters perform an immense disservice for the cause of conservation, and when people like the Cadzows are on the receiving end, the effect is doubly distressing, for their track record here is exemplary in its vision. He has so established the priorities for the pond, and so won over the other locals to his cause, that there is no reason why another century of swan broods should not rise from the island sanctuary. 'People around here are pretty super,' he said, 'as long as you do right by them.' I have heard some of the 'super' people express their own approval for the pleasures of such a sanctuary in their midst, for all the good things which rub off, consciously and unconsciously, from the proximity of swans. He has done right by them. Just don't call him a conservationist.

By early April, the house martins are back, slinging their own dark arrowheads across the pond, the first of the fork-tails. They have the pond's air to themselves a week or two before the place thickens with the chatter of swallows, the screech of swift. On April 5, the pen sat tight and stayed there. The Cadzows passed with a wave of greeting and a 'May 10!' prediction shouted from the car window. No bookie worth the name would give you odds against the eggs hatching out when the Cadzows reckon they'll hatch, although you might have got a price on a fourth consecutive clutch of nine with, according to Brian, the chance of a small accolade in the Guinness Book of Records. I scribbled down his prediction and admired his well-founded optimism. There was no reason not to be optimistic. He had stacked the odds so painstakingly in favour of the swans' success.

Fifty miles away, on the loch which lies beyond a certain flagship mountain of the southern Highlands, the odds are stacked the other way. The floods have come. The mountains seethe whitely, the snow melt swells the burns, and three weeks of rains are perfectly ill-timed to devastate the resident mutes' nesting ambitions. They swim over fences and gates and the river's burst banks, between the crowns of half-drowned trees. No shred of land suitable for a nest is visible. There is little food, for that too is half-drowned too far underwater for even a swan's neck. If memory plays a significant role in the lives of swans, these two must dread this season. The mystery is why, year after year, they undergo it all again. They alone will know.

It was the English naturalist Thomas Pennant who first distinguished formally the mute swan from the whooper and the Bewick (then still believed to be the same species), calling them 'tame swan' and 'wild swan'. He revised his ideas when he discovered in 1768 his 'tame' swan bred wild in Russia. It says much for the state of the infant Britain at the time that he knew more about Russia than Scotland. No whooper lives a wilder life than these mountain-hemmed mutes, and in the furthest-flung of Scotland's islands there are many mutes which live and nest through springs and summers of long and wild isolation. When Pennant revised his distinctions, changing 'tame' to 'mute', he sustained his reputation as an indifferent judge of swans. His mistake has not been totally eradicated even now. In Holland, for example, the whooper is still 'wilde zwann' and in France, 'cygne sauvage'.

Two days before the Cadzows' prediction was due to fulfil itself, I was driving back from Edinburgh and decided on the spur of the moment to divert the few miles to the pond. The May morning was hot and still and the cob was already on the pondside grass sunning himself. He was stretched full out, one wing partly extended, and he regarded my arrival with no flicker of any muscle save an eyelid which blinked open and closed again like a collie on a hearthrug. Eventually, he stood to preen.

His mate was restless on the nest, constantly shuffling and adjusting her position, and just as I was beginning to wonder about the prediction going the distance, the head of a cygnet, tiny, timid and grey, appeared in the middle of her back. She had begun to hatch. It was good to be there at that moment, to see the first cygnet's first glance at the perfect swan nursery, to acknowledge in the company of whatever benign spirit of swans presides over that place that life will never be better for that scrap of a swan than it was there and then, the world never more secure. To fumble up through the warm white fog of the deepest feathers and emerge standing on the back of a swan . . . there are worse ways to confront the world for the first time than that.

The peaceable nature of swans was at its most convincing that morning, the chocolate box clichés at their most seductive. Tree shadows and sunlight barred the back and neck of the pen where she sat with new life tugging and tumbling slowly beneath her. There was a sublime and almost perfect beauty about the moment, the setting and its focal point swan. The sun lit her the brightest of whites, so that she glowed, shining herself, especially on the small feathers of breast and belly which she worked at constantly. Through the glasses they looked more like ermine than feathers. Remember Tunnicliffe, and seen in that shining whitest light there is lemon in the shadows where they fall on her back, faintest flowing green on the back of her head where it is almost brushed by a weeping branch.

I am aware as I record the moment that there are those who will find it overdone, too vividly painted, the beauty overstated, the sense of perfection I feel misplaced. It is, after all, a common enough occurrence of nature, a biological certainty, more or less. Yet if you have watched swans for uncounted hundreds of hours and travelled hundreds of miles for the privilege, say, of watching them cross the Skye shore in September or carpet a loch in Easter Ross in their thousands, it is easy to come under the spell of swans and concede that there is more to my swan-watching than mere wildlife observation. But I am hardly unique in that.

English kings and queens were moved by the beauty of swans (what else?) to claim them as royal. Cygnus was the son of Neptune and was turned into a swan and placed in the heavens as a constellation of stars by Apollo, no less. The same Apollo had a chariot of swans (still does for all I know) in which he accompanied the birds' spring migration north. And for as long as we have known swans, we lesser mortals have folded them into the most precious and intimate accounts of our own occupation of the land, our folklore. And all this because we like the way swans look. We admire their beauty.

So when I sit alone by a pond I have watched for ten years because of its swans, and when I have been diverted there by chance two days too early, and I find that the first cygnet emerges while I sit there, and my passion for swans as wild theatre is lit by the most flattering of spotlights, and I have seen this particular spring through to its culmination two or three times a week, week after week since that first grey January day when the swans flew down to breast away a corner of ice-free water . . . when I accumulate all these in my mind, and add to their store the thirty years of iced ponds since that winter the Cadzows sledged rocks out to make an island and all their labourings in the cause of swans, what I saw on a hot May morning *was* sublime and the beauty of it *was* at least as perfect a definition of beauty as I have met in nature.

The Cadzows were not at home when I called, but Brian phoned that night to say she had hatched – eight. No record then, but good enough, we agreed. So two days later I was back with my camera, and the swans marshalled their eight preposterously appealing cygnets to the Cadzows' front door for a fistful of crumbs. Barbara Cadzow pronounced them the 'healthiest looking ever' and 'so un-nervous'. They swim in a well organised platoon, orderly as cavalry, the pen ahead, the cob to the rear, and in their discipline which is surely instinctive is the reason why – here at least – they mostly survive.

Compare mute swans with mallards. For while the cygnets cross the pond under escort with all the well-bred nonchalance of their race, a new young brood of ten mallards goes erratically and unstoppably berserk. They scatter over the water like marbles on ice, syrupy golden-brown bendy-toy creatures, but betrayed by black eye-striped aggro, dawn-till-dusk wreakers of tiny havocs, self perpetuating clockwork punks, bird symbols of the futility of the one-parent family in an environment which breeds big families. The duck has done all the incubating, all the nest repairs, all the hatching; she led them to the water (kicking them off the wall or out of the tree if necessary) where she does all the shepherding. As shepherds go, she makes a good duck.

The drakes, meanwhile, gather in groups about the pond, prattling on four-at-a-time in the manner of deaf old leather-chaired gentlemen at the club. Long after the cygnets are settled back on the island for the night, the duckling thugs are out making life hell for the burgeoning evening insect population on the water. They sprint and spin and stand and snap and snatch at everything within reach and much which is not, missing seven times out of ten. But for a two-day-old, three out of ten is a substantial performance and a telling lesson in the art of survival. There are *a lot* of mallards. Ah, if only it were that simple.

The following day, the brood of ten was down to three. The duck limped painfully away from a couch in the sun and took to the water, swimming clumsily. Three ducklings leapt from the reeds to her bidding and, Brian Cadzow told me, another brood of seven was reduced to one overnight. Fox, or cat, or both. Still, even a crippled mallard duck should be able to shepherd three ducklings safely, and perhaps that is enough of an average. There *are* a lot of mallards.

The swans have taken our food and she leads them off to the island. She climbs out and leaves the cygnets to their own devices. It is no easy climb up the rocks and through the nettles when you are four inches long and your wings are the size of a child's thumb. One makes it very quickly, long before the others, and I remember again the wild one last year, the one which flew first, and resolve to see if this brood would throw up such an adventurer too. Seven of the eight swarm up by a variety of routes, a three-feet high assault course of gullies and forests and encounters with spiders. The eighth, the Dopey of the brood, falls back from some impossible buttress by which time even the cob has caught up and stepped ashore. Dopey speeds for the cob's route and follows doggedly uphill, completely hidden by the tip of the cob's tail. It is a dangerous game, picking Disney names for swans. The story becomes confused. The dwarves become ugly ducklings, then Snow Whites.

The pen settles, the cygnets flock to her, and she casts out a wide wing for them to shelter under, as good a defence against a cooling north-west air as nature ever invented. Siesta is ruffled by the fast fly-pasts of first swallows.

Two days later I returned to the pond and found only seven cygnets but everything else apparently in order. I was unconcerned. Seven birds is still a comfortably above-average success rate, and the fact that there were realistic hopes for nine birds that year was an exclusively human ambition rather than anything nature may have had in mind. Still, it was the first casualty I'd ever heard of on the pond, and it would be worth a chat with the Cadzows. It could well have been nothing more ominous than another incident of the wing deformity which surfaced in a past brood, a genetically transmitted deficiency born in one of the adults. The solution is to remove the bird from the wild – it will never fly – as soon as the deformity is evident. The Cadzows were out, but I left convincing myself that that was all there was to it. As luck, or chance or whatever would have it, the opportunity to discuss the casualty did not arise for another ten days. When I did see them and the pond again, how everything had changed.

I have written earlier of a conspiracy of benevolent forces which hold sway over the pond, fuelling the swans' sustained success over many years. Now it was becoming clear that a rival and malevolent conspiracy had infiltrated the place. The first symptom of the coup was silence. There was not a young duck or grebe or moorhen or coot anywhere on the water. All that I could see were dozens of aimless, moping adults. Then I caught sight of the swans at the far end of the pond – the cob, the pen, and *two* cygnets, and I sensed the scent of small disaster.

Minutes later, the Cadzows began to unfold the grim story of the past two weeks. It had begun when the pipe which feeds the pond fractured, and over a few days, the water level fell so far that the cygnets were suddenly unable to negotiate the leap up the rocks to the island's night sanctuary. The cob would try time after time to coax them up, but the manœuvre was physically beyond them. So the adults led the brood to roost on the reedy shore, and it was there that night that the dog fox found them. The next morning there were seven, and I had come and gone and guessed nothing. Two days later there were six. The fox systematically reduced them to two before it was shot. The Cadzows felt as bereaved as the swans, and every day for a week they had gone to bed at night not knowing whether or not another swan would have died in the night. I thought later how a couple of months earlier we had looked out at the sitting pen and discussed enthusiastically the possibilities of the Guinness Book of Records with a fourth consecutive brood of nine. How trivial the idea suddenly seemed. I thought of the local worthy I had spoken to on my first night by this pond, ten years before, and his matter-of-fact boast that the swans raised seven birds every year. How cheerfully now would we all have settled for seven swans this year.

Mulling over the events of those few grim days, I was puzzled by two aspects of it all. One was why the swans did not resolve the problem for their cygnets by taking them up on to the island on their backs. Swans may not be the most intellectually gifted of birds, and at times their behaviour is downright baffling in the face of what seems an obviously more intelligent course of action to a non-swan. But you cannot cross-examine a swan, any more than you can calculate where intellect takes over from instinct and instinct from ritual. You can only watch and watch and watch, then guess. You can hardly expect a days-old cygnet to work out that by hitching a lift on an adult's back at a particular moment it would avoid a later situation which would endanger its life. Yet cygnets often travel on their parents' backs, presumably when they are tired or on a whim, or for safety or comfort, but apparently not in response to command. The Cadzows have resolved to build up an easier access to the island for next year, but I remain quite baffled by the fact that the swans did not provide it themselves.

The other troubling aspect of the brood's ill fortunes is that having taken the cygnets to roost on the shore, and therefore a situation of much less security, the adults could not defend their young against a single fox. I have watched swans drive off a large dog, even a fisherman's boat, and this self-same West Lothian cob had charged Barbara Cadzow – clearly identifiable as an ally and a hand that feeds – when she was caught inadvertently between the cob and the cygnets. Caught off balance, the force of the charge knocked her over. So why not drive off a fox, and for that matter, why would a fox tackle such a ferocious defender of its young anyway with the pondside's other richer and easier pickings?

Two answers suggested themselves. One is that the swan is inefficient in the dark, either unconfident of movement, or its eyesight is not as good as it is in daylight. It is an uncomfortable theory. Grazing whoopers, for example, often feed long after dark and fly unerringly to roost on the blackest of nights. My second theory is that these particular swans were so immune from danger on the pond's island and so dominant a force on the pond itself that their wild instincts were actually dulled, and their vigilance impaired. It still does not explain why, having lost one cygnet and then another within forty-eight hours, the adults did not try either to defend them more vigorously or move them somewhere safer. As it was, it took the repair of the pipe and the rise of the water level to stop the systematic killing of the brood. Killing the fox was only the first step. It would be a question of time, and very little time at that, before the dead beast's territory was taken over. So the swans and the two survivors regained the evening sanctuary of the island.

Even so, the fox and the pipe and the swans were only part of the story. Whether by accident, design, or an equally implausible alliance of predators, the pond was discovered by both mink and gulls at the same time. Mink are as fluent in water as out of it, and their presence in such a place of teeming wildfowl life is a threat of incalculable proportions. Reasonably enough from the mink's point of view, they began by killing the easiest targets, the young birds, dozens of them, less than a month old. The Cadzows called in expert help and the mink presence was swiftly halted, but not before they had made a telling impact on the population of the pond. And how long before more mink move in?

That still leaves the gulls. They fly in from a new reclamation project a mile away where land is being filled in by tipping. The refuse attracts the gulls in vast numbers, and a few of them, black-backs and black-heads, have stumbled on the helplessness of the youngest ducklings.

'You see them land on the water, snatch a duckling, then fly off with it and another gull chases it across the pond trying to persuade it to drop the duckling. But what can you do?' The reclamation project may take two more years of dumping and gulls.

He surveys the pond where a single coot chick is the only visible young bird. It is perhaps two days old, and wears the comical bloody-nosed mask of all young coots. I used to smile at their appearance. Now I watch it and wonder how long it has to live.

Brian Cadzow asks again, with a bewildered shake of the head: 'What can you do when nature decides to act in such a perverse fashion?'

The last few weeks have hit them both hard. So easily is a swan's paradise lost.

Yet, at the end of the day, it is the human observers who feel the loss most keenly. Nature is interested in species, not individual survivals. The swans will have a leisurely summer rather than their normal arduous one. There will be flying lessons for two, come September, and the pond's future swan generations will not have the problem of low water access to the island. The gulls will go when the tip closes. Besides, in any small sanctuary like the pond where wildfowl flourish so conspicuously there are bound to be smoke signals to predators. What matters is that the sanctuary is effective enough and productive enough to blunt the predators' tooth and claw. The Cadzows have seen to it that over the years, the swans and all the pond's lesser tribes have prospered. One lean year out of so many is no failure, and nature is not renowned for perpetual perversity. It is a great service the pair of them have performed here for swans, and one flawed season only highlights the worth of their achievement.

It is the last week in June. Under the mountain fifty miles away, the pen still sits on. Now she is late, even for her third nest, and it has rained ominously for two weeks.

5

Swans on the Highland Edge

HALFWAY BETWEEN the pond swans and the mountain loch swans a small reservoir lies under a mile of crag. A dull sea of plantation spruce, a woodland regime of stultifying boredom, has crept across the moorland hills towards the water over the last fifteen years, though the face of the crag and a clutch of small ungrazed islands show the way things used to be – a forest order dominated by Scots pine, well laced with birch, rowan, ash, sycamore, willow, oak. A path threads uneasily between the old woodland and the new, then abruptly climbs and sheds them both. The water is suddenly unscreened and, far below your feet, the old pines and a smattering of larches crampon up the crag, the highest of them flayed wide and low by the wind. The surprise of the place is the mountains. They startle up out of the foothills twenty miles to the north-west, a saw-tooth arc of the horizon, uncompromising southernmost rampart of the Highlands. At the heart of the wide flat realm, neither Highland nor low, between the crag and the northern foothills is one of the great landmarks of all Scotland, all its history and all its landscapes, the Stirling Castle rock. The view from the summit of the crag is of a watershed of landscapes. 'Stirling', they used to say, 'is the buckle that clasps Highland and Lowland thegither'. Certainly, however you cross the wide and flat-bottomed Carse of Stirling you emerge on the far side into a transformed landscape.

In this book's north-westering journey, it is on the Carse that you first encounter whooper swans. They come in October, thicken the first small and wary flocks in the grazing fields in November, then scatter across the winter face of the land. It is a land I know better than most for I have lived with its castle rock and its mountain skyline for twenty-and-more restless years. In all that time, the autumn return of the whoopers has been a reunion I celebrate, its significance deepening with the years, symbolic of my own journeyings along every compass point. For the Carse is that kind of place, a hub among landscapes. I cannot remember the first time I became aware of them as seasonal neighbours, but the memory of the most vivid encounter is undimmed years after the event. The power of it equals the mutes in their Edinburgh street, but it is the more telling because, as far as anyone can manipulate nature, I set it up.

I walked the track between the woods on a December evening floodlit by a big moon. The remnants of an early snowfall patched the moors and clung to an old rut in the track and wedged in the highest rock of the crag. The gliding cross of a magpie over the track was a moving fragment of a pied landscape. As the track begins to climb it is already a hundred feet above the water and well screened by dense woodland, so that a small knot of whooper swans advertised themselves by sound rather than sight. They were huddled close under the trees at the south end of the loch, the quiet bugling of their voices a rich-vowelled and muted variant on the far-carrying flight call, but their subdued conversation had the night's midwinter stillness to itself and I heard every syllable as clearly as my own footfall. I descended through the trees on a roe deer track, diverted widely enough to come to the water's edge perhaps a hundred yards from the centre of the sound, and immediately confounded my best efforts by underestimating the size of the gathering. What I had taken to be half a dozen birds was a flock of nearer twenty, the nearest of them much too close to my line of approach. They saw me seconds before I saw them, and I emerged from the trees to watch them swim away across the small bay.

There was, for all that, a profound beauty in their going, with the moonlight full on them, delineating heads and necks against the unfathomable black of the trees glinting on the birds' small wakes as they swam. I stayed where I was for an hour, by which time the birds had settled again and reverted to a persistent companionable muttering while long skeins of geese crossed the loch in the direction of a second loch higher up on the moor. It was as I listened to the geese flying down the same groove in the air, flight after flight of them, that I concocted the circumstances which would provide one extraordinary encounter with the whoopers and become the basis of a winter ritual.

The north shore of the loch is a dam. Beyond the dam, the land falls steeply to a small wooded valley. The water which courses through the valley, and which feeds the reservoir, bears a famous name. It is a douce enough water now, but once, on a June day in 1314, it flowed red and put a revered name on the lips of every Scot who was ever born from that day to this; for this is the Bannock Burn. Among its lesser claims to fame is that where its valley leaves the hills is a flightpath for hundreds of greylag and pinkfooted geese, and for small flights of whooper swans. I reasoned as I watched the geese through that moonlight night that the swans would fly in by the same route. I also reasoned that if some of them at least were roosting on the reservoir (others fly on to the high moorland loch) they would probably be descending by the time they crossed the dam. If I chose a dull and cloudy night and settled myself on the dam in the dusk it should be possible to get very close to flying whoopers. The dull night was for my own convenience – not so cold and not so long a wait, because the birds stay out feeding longer after dark on the frost-clear moon-strewn nights.

Three nights later I wandered the crag in the late afternoon, watched a buzzard flirt with the airs which buffet a weird little phallic parliament of sandstone pillars, scanned the water far below for its wintering gatherings of wigeon, goldeneye, goosander, tufted ducks and interminable mallards. Three herons rasped in the bay. A roe doe barked at my back. Jackdaws skipped about the sky and the crag and tormented the buzzard. A goosander drake took the dam like a hurdler. The drakes are big, striking birds, especially in flight when the vivid red bill thrusts through the air like a bowsprit. Dark green head and creamy flanks and white wings follow in an elongated slender and hunched profile which suggests (if your imagination runs to the same quirks as mine does) a duck which has been wrung through a cartoonist's mangle. I can visualise a Tom and Jerry animator giggling with a mallard duck, feeding it into a mangle, and watching it emerge as a goosander.

The flat top and back of the dam are turf. A stone wall protects the drop into the water. I crossed to the middle of the dam, settled myself against the wall, opened the coffee flask and the whisky flask, unwrapped a few squares of chocolate, and prepared to get cold as slowly as possible. It was five o'clock, it had been dark for half an hour, and the first geese were already in. Within an hour I was shivering and I had been rewarded with two mallards and one merganser which flew so close over my head and emerged so suddenly from the gloom that I was momentarily terrified. What madness is this, just to see a familiar bird in an unfamiliar light? What for? What was the point? Why don't I get a proper job? There is nothing like discomfort to test any naturalist's dedication and stamina. It is as well to know that there is also nothing like discomfort to enhance the indelible moments which last you a lifetime. In fact, they tend not to last you a lifetime if you haven't worked for them.

I heard the swans before I saw them. At the first meandering sound I began to strain at the dark. There is no way of knowing where or how far away they will appear in this absence of light, and the vagueness of the sound straddling a wide flight of perhaps a dozen birds is impossible to pin down. The sound came on. But surely it was too low? It seemed to get dragged down into the conifer woodlands which thronged the bottom of the dam fifty feet below me. I had expected something 200 feet higher. Then the darkness parted and the birds were there, a wide vee of thirteen, ranged in six and seven behind a front-runner, and no more than a hundred yards away. There had been no obstacle in their path to prevent me from seeing them other than the absence of light. Now they simply came within range of my vision and were suddenly present. It was as if they had just been switched on, vaguely luminous, or placed in the air before me.

I had to make two immediate adjustments. One was psychological, for I had set my mind to cope with a descending skein which would appear as silhouettes against the sky. Instead they were pale against the depths of the forest, becoming as vivid as the patched snow, and I was looking down across their spreadeagled backs. My mind's eye had seen swans in the relaxed glide of landing. Now my eyes saw the attitude of flight transform as it prepared for the baulking wall of the dam. Wingstrokes deepened and heightened, the pulse of them unchanged, and I knew again the awesome relentlessness of swan flight. The birds' throats belled loudly on the winter night.

The second adjustment was the physical one of eyesight. I was looking in the wrong place until just a hint of movement below dragged my eyes down from the sky. At first the shapes which emerged were unfathomable blurs so that moments elapsed before my eyes could harden them into swans and count them. My head swam with these somersaults of mind and eye as the birds came on.

When they reached the foot of the dam I saw one bird 'refuse', like a stage-frightened showjumper, and peel off sideways. I left it to its fate for the moment, such was the collective spell of the skein as they heaved up the air yards short of the dam. I was quite unprepared for the steepness of the climb. One moment I was looking down at the topside of their wings, the next the birds tilted and I saw the thin line of the wings' leading edge and the head-on wedges of yellow-and-black bills, and then the undersides and stowed undercarriage rushed past as they crossed the dam at ten feet. The leading bird passed perhaps twenty feet to my right; the second on his right flew directly over me and its passing wing thrust sent a rush of cold air about my face. A wave of white wings overwhelmed the dam and the brassy clamour of whooper flight calls bounced from the cold stone at my back and sounded a din in my ears that left me dazed.

I moved for the first time, stood and turned to look back after the swans as they crossed the water. The loch was a startling bowl of pale light after two unbroken hours watching dark crag and forest grow darker. The birds stalled and glided and splashed down halfway across the loch, and with their landing and the steady diminuendo of their voices a heavy 'peace came dropping slow'. I thrilled to it all, an ecstasy held in check by an innate respect for the peace, so that instead of, say, shouting aloud, the exultation was pushed deeper within me. There it remains, and each winter dusk that I sit on the dam, it rekindles. It survives so well partly because the whole thing was plotted, because the element of surprise exceeded every conceivable expectation, and because although I sat openly and unscreened on the dam, I was a shadow on a wall of shadows and the birds flew by obliviously. The moment was, I think, the one where I felt, however fleetingly, a triumphantly unexceptional fragment of the swans' perception of the landscape. For the swan-watcher, there is no higher prize.

A single whooper note sounded behind me, a monosyllabic bugle call. 'Whoop!' it sang, but almost short enough to be pizzicato. I remembered the swan which had refused the dam, and saw nature throw a comic twist into its finest hour. The bird had landed low on a steep flank of the valley, and confounded by the narrowness of the valley, a nearby fence and a complete absence of room for manœuvre (for a swan take-off is a long and laborious and die-straight process), she was pointedly walking up the sheerest slopes of a field which dips abruptly down to the burn. Her only footholds were well-muddied cattle tracks, and up these she slapped her great webs, looking altogether preposterous. A swan on foot is never at its best, but a swan walking steeply uphill is a cruel parody of that natural grace which imbues every other aspect of swan behaviour. It was a tortuous ascent with many sideways diversions round whins and gradients that were too steep. False steps were retrieved by hastily opened wings, the walking swan's equivalent of the tightrope-walker's pole. Eventually she reached the crown of the field at which point she was slightly higher than the top of the dam's stone wall. She ran a dozen downhill paces with wings flexing, flew in a brief glide, landed on the water within yards of the dam, and as if she completely distrusted the medium of air, swam the half mile of loch to join the others. She was, inevitably, a young bird in her first winter, and for all that she had made her first migratory flight from Iceland, there was clearly a lot about the wiles of swanflight which she had yet to learn.

Each time I sit on the dam, I watch for the one that refuses the hurdle, but they never again came in so low, and never again have I seen a whooper swan lose its nerve.

If I was accustomed to mark my travels across the landscape like a slug, betraying every twist and turn and beeline, I would have worn a network of grooves across the Carse of Stirling. The Carse is the Forth's flat-bottomed valley, but it curls up at the edges to the south, the west and the north where hill and mountain gather round. Even the eastern end is barricaded in by the narrowest cross-section of the Ochil Hills, the Abbey Craig with the dire Victorian Wallace Monument inflicted on its woody dome, and the Castle Rock itself, wedged like a stopper in the neck of the valley. The Forth only escapes such a noose by writhing through a berserk course, a dozen of the maddest water miles in the country. But out in the heart of the Carse, there is little to lure your eyes east. The mountains signal the beginning and the end of the Highlands, from south-west to north, and as the sun puts down behind them at every season of the year, it is a compelling land and sky – a sky of almost Orcadian dimensions – which drapes across the Highland horizon. The Carse is a curious realm too with its own unique imprint, a legacy perhaps of the histories which have stamped the land and which lie stored just below its well-tilled surface. Much of it is drained bog, reclaimed sea loch, the corpse of a glacier. Flanders Moss (where the Carse begins to edge uphill towards the Lake of Menteith) is a souvenir of the landscape that was, all fickle bog and scrub woodland, and which somehow escaped the Carse's zealous agricultural reforms. It thrums with wildlife at every season.

I am a fretful and uneasy townsman, even in such a distinguished town as Stirling, and the Carse has habitually been my decompression chamber, where I breathe a freer air and put on my true clothes. It is no coincidence that at the end of many of those trails I have worn across the Carse lies a field or a watersheet well used by swans, for in their company are many civilising influences. It is in these few doorstep square miles under their skylining mountains that I have driven and walked time and again, thousands of miles by now, to watch swans at close quarter, to watch what they do, and to wonder why they do it, to wonder why men made such an uncharacteristically enlightened choice of a wild creature to guard their souls and adorn their folklore.

Even where the Carse relents and my grooved trail threads the first pass of the southern Highlands, there lies a beautiful loch where mute swans nest in the shadow of the mountains. The Lake of Menteith at the west end of the Carse is the wildfowl hub of that land. Autumn and early spring it fires vast salvoes of greylag and pink-footed geese into the dawn, a spectacle of sound and wings which darkens the sky just as it had begun to lighten. It might be 8,000 birds, more or less at once. Twenty or thirty or more whooper swans go with them. At dusk, they all return, long scribbles of birds, the geese following the tens of thousands of gulls, the swans usually the last to fly in to roost beating across the lochside trees, angling down so far out across the water that you often lose them before they land. Oh, the sound of all those throats! The autumn speech of wild geese under a mountain skyline, layered with the deeper grace notes of whoopers, is a cacophany of peace, especially if, like me, you incline to the dusk variations on the theme rather than the dawn. Dawn dispatches the geese in a single stunning explosion, followed by a day-long silence;

the dusk weeds them out, lures them home subtly in ones and twos and tens and hundreds, and everything in between; they come in over the mountains, the trees, the shrouded east at your back, and they land and settle in a thick line across a mile of the water and there they gossip all night about the day and its doings, the night and its dangers. It is a long and lovely finale to any autumn or winter day, and there is as much of it as you want. You can stay and listen and watch for as long as you can endure a winter night on the Highland edge. The sky fire is long dowsed. Ben Lomond, which drapes a long shoulder over the loch's north-western corner, is an inked-in mountain, and just as you think the day is done, then the wind throws you a brassy snatch of homing whooper. You try to pinpoint the place where they will appear. The most wrong that I have been is 180 degrees; I mutter, 'Danger, naturalist at work,' and I think the last swan is laughing at me. It's salutary, and my feathers rarely stay ruffled for long, not in this company.

I have been known to go to bizarre lengths to see such spectacle at its utmost, pursuing a wildlife philosophy which is the antithesis of twitching. The twitcher travels to see a single bird once, to pronounce it seen. I travel to see that with which I am already intimately acquainted but to see it again in a different light, to pronounce it seen more clearly or more profoundly, or just more. It was in such a spirit that I drove through one of the foulest days November can muster (and in northern Scotland November can muster more of the foulest things in nature than most places) to a loch near the Buchan shore high on Scotland's north-east shoulder. At that time of year, the whoopers traditionally gather in their hundreds, 600 to 700 in a good year, and geese in substantial five-figure hordes where the first of the five is not always a one. It had seemed a good idea at the time.

So I drove for half a day through whitening summits and traipsed for a sodden hour to an unlovely corner of the Buchan coast where, for reasons best known to themselves, the hordes fall from the late afternoon skies to roost. The height of the day's ambition was to see the biggest armada of swans of my life. Ten whoopers crossed my path a mile from the loch, which seemed a good omen, but they proved to be the last swans I saw in flight until after dark. A dozen scattered desultorily about the loch itself, a dozen more mute swans kept them company. In the middle of the water there was a pack of coots so dense you could hardly see water through the mass. Counting them was hopelessly haphazard in the turgid light of noon flayed by sleety squalls on the sea wind. Twelve hundred was a reasonable assessment. The light began to fail at about 3 p.m. and the day and the journey seemed doomed to dismal, drab and depressing disappointment. But nature's saving graces rarely bypass patient vigils completely and no one with half an eye and a tolerable immunity to sitting and shivering it out through a few sodden, grey and half-dark hours will see nothing. The vigil was attended first by a short-eared owl which came curious enough and close enough to fill the glasses directly overhead. A persistent wheezy monosyllable betrayed a young bird on a fence-post fifty yards away, and in the hour before the geese began to home in on the loch, there were four owls ghosting and stalling and falling on some hapless Buchan vole's last gasp.

The first skein of geese was a thousand strong and they came out of the north-west where the sky was at its palest, a shade of light black, the sound of them a fanfare such as a demented and hideously oversubscribed accordion band might perform. They wheeled in on a storm of windsong, that phenomenon of goose flight when the skein's formation collapses into a shambles of individuals crazily spilling air from their wings, whiffling down to a thousand giddy landings. The coot raft took to its heels at this, and sped over the surface in a solid stain to land 300 yards away, their flying a pointed reminder that there was nothing in the trails of the geese or the glowering skies which even approximated to the true black. In the company of coots on such a day there are only shades of grey for comparisons. They would shift twice more in the next half hour as the goose rain fell and fell, but settled eventually for the fact that so many geese in so little water left no hiding place. Soon there was little clear water to flee to so they simply sat blackly on and tholed the clamour as it grew and grew.

The geese piled in now, every few minutes a few hundred more – by my best guess about 12,000 pinkfeet in the space of an hour and a half, although those I missed as the light flew might have added two thousand more. It was the last of them, though, flying down the pitch darkness, which freed from time's snare a long captive and unsuspected memory. It was a small skein, and unlike the rest, it came in from the sea where the sky was almost coot-black and the birds invisible. I was aware first of a profound sense of dislocation, robbed not just of familiar landmarks but any landmarks at all, and in the worsening weather and the almost perversely solitary nature of the expedition, I felt suddenly and acutely alone. I clung, desperate for a consoling presence, to the haunting approach of the unseen geese down the night sky, my one familiar reference point. The sound, now that I isolated it in my mind from all the loch's wildfowl bustle, pitched me back thirty-five years to childhood winters on the edge of the Tay estuary. Suddenly I was a seven-year-old, skidding on frosted pavements while walking home under the stars from Sunday tea at Aunty Meg's. The carol of the geese, the haloed sheen of gas street-lights, and my father's side were a trilogy of benevolent forces in which I delighted. For a few seconds by a lochside in Buchan, where I had never stood before and have not since, too cold and too alone for comfort, the wild geese spun me a chrysalis of childhood well-being.

A deeper bugle sounded, dispelling the moment. The darkness offered up sixty-two whooper swans. I watched them land a dozen yards away and thrilled to them as I always do for their uncompromis-ing wildness and their easy way with the far north of the world. I remembered then why I had come. If the journey in search of a swan armada could hardly be said to have achieved its purpose, I had made a richer discovery. It was the recognition that my own instinctive inclination towards the northlands of the world and their wild bird hordes was rooted in the rich seedbed of my own childhood; that my work now as a nature writer stemmed from the same root and was not, as I had so often uneasily imagined, a rootless acquisition. The continuity of Scottish tradition has always held profound significance for me, and suddenly I was aware of my own secure place in that tradition. It was a telling hour of my life. My dark mood was banished then and there with the geese. It all explained, too, my passion for whooper swans, and through them all swans, with brilliant clarity, for the swans are merely variations on the same theme as the geese, and I simply crossed their path later in life. In the same moment, the nature writer's bond with nature was immeasurably strengthened. Sixty-two incoming whoopers, even in the dark, amount to a mighty consolation, and I left that shore finally satisfied that the spectacle is in the swan itself, that sixty or six hundred swans are no more exquisite, no more perfect a creation than six swans, or one. It was a long way to go to discover such a simplistic truth.

The darkness around me was suddenly full of wings, blacker than the night, frantic after the leisured ease of the swans' sudden appearance. It was the coots. They too had tholed enough of this water, and were leaving.

The geese and the swans begin to mass in late October, until by mid-November their favourite age-old reunion haunts seethe. Then they begin to disperse across the face of the land until they regroup in the early spring and depart piecemeal for the northlands. The geese might muster 8,000 on the Lake of Menteith by November, the swans rarely more than fifty, but on a late October day, the lake's swans have found a wide flat stubble field to their liking and come coursing in on the wind, loudly exuberant, the Arctic on their wings, or so it always seems to me. I counted them as they landed, a reflex action which serves no real purpose as far as I am concerned, except that I can occasionally dine out on the biggest flocks, for numbers seem somehow to obsess wildfowl aficionados. Once out here I saw 2,000 pinkfeet in a single field, and one snow goose. For four hours, I did not take my eyes off the snow goose, except that when the flock rose and moved 200 yards I followed them and settled myself again where I could watch the one white bird. Spectacle in nature is what you make of it.

So my fifty whoopers bounced exuberantly down to feed, and the lowest morning sun caught them and their arctic-ness was a small white blaze in the bleached fawns of the stubbles. I watched from my car, which is as good a hide as any out on such a low-profile landscape where cover is minimal and the birds wary. Winter swans are as sociable as they are vigorously solitary during the nesting season, and these fifty pinned to the field like a brooch would beckon all that morning's swans to join them, and through the morning they came, small skeins from the small lochs in the low hills above the Carse, or further-flung travellers from Loch Leven thirty miles to the east. They are great travellers, whooper swans, and ornithologist Valerie Thom's great work, *Birds in Scotland*, details the following remarkable journey of a marked swan:

One marked in Iceland on 25 July was at Loch Eye [Easter Ross] on 15 October, the Loch of Strathbeg [Aberdeenshire] on 1 November,

Caerlaverock [Dumfriesshire] from 30 November to 2 December, and the Ouse Washes [Cambridgeshire] from 7 December to 12 March. It was in Caithness by 25 March and was back in Iceland by 19 May.

Within these prodigious distances there would be daily flights to feed. The surest sign of good feeding for a group of swans is the sight of another flock already eating. In a landscape like the Carse, such a feeding flock will be conspicuous from miles away, and as more swans arrive in the area, a small feeding flock can swell dramatically over a period of days. The field before me, which now held its tight knot of fifty birds, has had swans in it every day for the past two weeks. Six arrived on October 6, and had the place to themselves for a week. Then there were ten for three days, then twenty-two. Suddenly there were fifty arriving as a single flock, and putting their mark on the land. By noon there were ninety-four, and that portion of the field they had defined for themselves was becoming distinctly crowded. It was bounded to the west by a hedge which obscured the farmland immediately beyond and prevented me from seeing what had been happening there all morning. Suddenly a new flock appeared so low over the hedge that they must surely have been in the next field. They came so thick and fast that I quickly lost count, and waited for the mass of birds to readjust itself. The new arrivals numbered 104, the whole flock 198.

I was not the only one who had noticed the deluge. A Volvo pulled up, a window slid down, and the face of a farmer grimaced, first at me, then at the swans.

'So how do I get rid of the buggers?' he asked.

'You could flit,' I suggested, catching a less than malicious note in his voice.

'Any ideas where?'

'Iceland's vacant, until May anyway.'

'Aye, I suppose it could be worse, we could have them here in the summer, eh?'

'What *do* you do about them?' I asked.

'Not much. Count them. Chase them off after a while sometimes, if I think I'm getting more than my share. But we could spend all autumn and winter shifting them around, them and the geese. I like the swans – we had two hundred and thirteen yesterday – but there's some chaps have very old-fashioned ideas about frightening them off.'

'Like what, shooting?'

'I didn't say that. If you get fed up watching them, see if you can shift them.'

He was gone, leaning on the horn, a gesture which left the swans quite unmoved.

A deep calm, almost as visible as a cloud, settled on the midday flock. A few grazed on, but many sat and dozed or preened half-heartedly, keeping the machinery of the plumage ticking over. Many more just sat, a posture which reduces the shape of a head-on swan to an elemental simplicity – a low, wide dome from the crown of which protrudes a ramrod neck topped with a wedge-shaped head. I tried to sketch it again and again, but unaccomplished artist that I am, I could make nothing of its perfect symmetrical simplicity.

There is, I realised then, a crucial difference between whoopers and mute swans in winter flocks. The mutes remain a loosely sociable assembly of individuals, but the whoopers behave as a concerted flock, capable of reaching collective decisions and acting on them. I have often watched whoopers signal approaching danger, transmit aware-ness of it through the flock, assess the degrees of danger, decide whether to fly or stay and act accordingly. Now I watched it stir, a breath of awareness which went through the flock like a ripple on a pool, the apparently imperturbable nature of the calm revealed as nothing more than a thin veneer cloaking a perpetual state of aware-ness. As the new mood went through the flock it raised dozing heads and brought sitting birds to their feet.

The problem seemed to be in the west. Although I could find nothing with the glasses, I thought perhaps a hen harrier was scouring the edge of the field. The harrier is a bird which always troubles swans, although I cannot imagine how it could be perceived as a threat: perhaps the inherent sense of menace in the slowness of the hunting flight is simply an unnerving presence. No other bird seemed troubled bar the swans, but troubled undoubtedly they were. Their questioning 'woo-pah?' calls spread through the flock, a clear interro-gatory edge to the second syllable. Slowly the flock relaxed, and every bird sat, and just as I had assumed that the danger had passed, every head shot up again, several birds stood, and the calls once more gave voice to a collective anxiety. Still there was nothing for me to see or hear. The birds sat again, but when, within minutes, they were back on their feet, there was no mistaking the problem, for this time the alarm coincided with a peal of thunder. They had been responding to it while it was still beyond my own hearing.

The sky fell, the mountains vanished, and the storm advanced as a grey wall obliterating landmarks. The first lightning seared the air, but produced no visible response in the swans. Then, as the thunder neared and the rain thudded down, there came a real sense of fear through the flock. Every peal produced the same shocked response, but there was no attempt to seek cover or fly. At its height, the storm grounded every flying thing on the Carse. The air had been giddy with rooks, wood pigeons, vast movements of pinkfeet, the hedges thrumming with small bird sound. Now all that I could see was the swan flock, every head tilted high as a diver's into the rain, the attitude only broken for a few seconds while birds rubbed their bills on their breasts again and again, a gesture I simply could not understand. Long after the storm had passed, they were staring anxiously after it, the receding thunder still carrying to their ears long after it had passed beyond the reach of mine.

The rooks were instantly airborne again, and suddenly every swan was standing tall and flexing wings and shaking and reordering plumage and grooming, a process of great vigour almost gleeful in its vitality, as much a response of relief as anything.

Then they walked down to a lower level of the field as the sun speared through, and there they began visibly to relax. One thing intrigued me as I considered their behaviour during the storm. It was that they had been utterly indifferent to repeated shafts of lightning, so much so that I wonder if they actually saw the lightning at all. Yet they were so obviously discomfited by thunder – a strange response when you consider that lightning is the real threat while thunder is not.

The unmistakable song of a yellowhammer lightened the oppressive aftermath of the storm. It carried the vigour of a lightly coiled spring unfurling, the pitch of it rising in fractions of semi-tones note-by-note until, with one last monosyllabic flourish, the spring reached the end of its tether and slipped back to the starting note. It was a call as charismatic as the bird itself. The male stood, a small yellow blaze perched on a hawthorn stem, as breathtakingly bright on the hedge's muted backcloth as a kingfisher on a dark stream. I moved too suddenly for his singing comfort, though, and as he flew, he took two others with him that I hadn't seen. The small triangle of their flight and landing twenty yards away was a wedge of colour adrift on the air, a low kite impaled on a hawthorn hedge.

In many parts of Scotland the bird is still called the yellayite, and in a few more there are very localised versions on the theme of 'yorlin', including yoldrin, yaldrin, yarlin, yeldrin and yirlin, any or all of which can have a 'yellow' prefix. What no source explains is what any of the words mean, or for that matter, why 'hammer'? Still, the thin music of a solitary yorlin can sound like a symphony in the first ten minutes after a thunderstorm.

A new sound came on that still laden air, a vast whisper which became a roar, and grew until the air felt swollen with it. It was the work of geese, but it presented itself as something weirdly disembodied. For fully thirty seconds while the sound welled there was no sight of the birds at all. Then the first of them emerged from a far field, well screened by trees, and lifted into the sky. The sound was not just of voices but also of wings, and from the first it was obvious that a great host of birds was on the move. Soon I began to see how great.

The first thousand crossed the trees tight as a cloud, and as soon as they cleared the woodland barrier the noise level rose appallingly. The mass of them began to cut diagonally across the swans' field, as if a banner of incomprehensible proportions was being towed aloft. By the time the first birds had covered half a mile, the hordes at their back still rose from the hidden field beyond the trees. By the time the last of them were airborne, the first birds had travelled a mile and started to circle back to land in a field beyond the swans. Now the flock began to curve and the leading birds were seen through the mass which followed them. The effect was to deepen the great darkness of the mass in the way that an artist draws deeper shadows by cross-hatching pencil strokes. I had cross-hatching geese, a dense mile of 6,000 pinkfeet. Following the flight of a single bird in that chaos was simply impossible, and such was the press of them that they might all have been ink black instead of brown and grey and pink and white.

Any flock of geese is a frantic thing when it lands and the formation of flight disintegrates into a dizzying spiral of individuals. A mile of birds does not land all at once, of course, but they rained down on that single field with all the relentlessness of the storm which had just crossed their path. I wondered if the Volvo-driving farmer was watching them; would he feel that this was 'more than his share'? And how would he feel about stepping out into that field to put 6,000 birds, each the size of a goose, into the air with the mad roar of them about his head? I'm not sure that I would envy him his role as the still centre of such a whirlpool of nature.

The sight and sound of the geese died as they landed, screened and silenced again by hedges and trees, leaving an uncanny vacuum about their flightpath. I filled it by easing down the side of the hawthorn hedge towards the swans. When I had a clear sightline to them again they had reassumed that veneer of calm. Most of the birds were sitting, some of them coiled into shapelessness with their necks laid down one flank, an attitude which gave them the appearance of a random scattering of cushions. A few birds fed, conversation reduced to occasional soft monosyllables. Nature contrives no more perfect illusion of peace than a flock of resting whooper swans. It is a wonderfully convincing sham, hair-triggered. Hare-triggered too. A big brown buck loped down the field and with a clear hundred yards of swan-free land on either side of the flock, chose to lope right through it. Necks stiffened, heads swivelled, sitting birds stood, for a big buck like this one could stand twice as tall as a cushioned swan. No hostilities were exchanged beyond troubled glares and glances. Perhaps the hare was making a territorial point, being a twelve-month resident. Perhaps he knew the peaceable nature of winter whoopers. Perhaps he was just lucky. If there had been a handful of mute swans keeping the company of the whoopers (as often there were in winter flocks) the hare's luck might have been stretched. As it was, he soft-shoed through the flock and the hedge beyond, and the birds stood stiffly and let him through, like Moses parting the Red Sea.

I left the flock in its beautiful becalmed state. Perhaps some of them would throw a well-drilled brass band across the dam that evening, and we would meet again and pass again. The restlessness of whoopers is no more than my own; where they fly I follow and watch and wait and learn, and sometimes they divert my attention away from them by throwing a mile of geese across their scent. But it never works for long.

My winters on the Carse are well punctuated with whooper encounters, many of them chance encounters, many more of them planned. Planning to meet swans is only possible, of course, because (certainly in terms of winter feeding grounds) they are creatures of habit. Anyone who drives north-west from Stirling to Callander and the Highlands beyond in the last few weeks of winter and the first of spring will pass a roadside field where swans gather year after year, and where they are persuaded to linger by good grazing and a benevolent farmer. The constant din of traffic a hundred yards away does not divert them or cause them a moment's disturbance, but park by the field gate in full view of them and they are instantly on full alert and walking pointedly away from you. By habit and repute I use a farm track some distance from their preferred grazing areas and on the low edge of what appears to be a flat field. But like so many of the Carse's fields their flatness is a cloak for small contours just pronounced enough to hide a dozen swans at 200 yards. So I park, and sooner or later the grazing heads will cross that fold in the ground and step leisurely down into my half of the field. The car is already there, a familiar presence, a piece of the field edge. In this way, the birds simply walk themselves into my field of vision, a strategy of supreme simplicity with the twin flaws that sometimes it can take them two or three hours to cross the fold, and sometimes they just don't cross it at all.

It worked flawlessly, though, on a late afternoon in late March. The evenings have begun to lengthen conspicuously by then, and nightfall begins to edge past seven o'clock. Two hours before that, I had slipped the car quietly into the track and parked, and within ten minutes the heads, then the necks, then whole swans, were bridging the highest part of the field. Seventy-one swans formed a ragged line a hundred yards long, the heart of the flock directly under the skyline shape of Ben Lomond. Three days of rain had finally abated, and as the sun showed briefly just above the mountain, it put an intense blush on tiered banks of cumulus. The swans, the mountain, the pink and powerful sky, looked like an overdone stage set, in which the director couldn't resist just one more spectacular effect. Any minute now I expected the mile of geese to re-emerge and fly across the sun in a grotesque parody of a Peter Scott painting, or a rainbow arch flung over the mountain for the swans to fly through. But it was a heady enough hour as it was, and I settled the glasses on the top of the partially lowered car window and focused on the swans. While I watched, the sun spilled a shaft down the field and sent it swinging across the ground as fast as a ballroom spotlight. It caught the swans at one end of the line, and for perhaps twenty seconds the last eight birds were flamingos while the rest stayed untransformed. Then the light was gone from them and order was restored. But the phenomenon was not done. A dozen times in the next twenty minutes the sun pushed away a patch of cloud and hurtled down another moving light, and struck the same uncanny pink shade on a group of swans before switching it off again.

Just as abruptly the sun forsook the swans and started to play among the old snow patches on Ben Lomond. These too turned pink so that the mountain glowed. An old derivation of the mountain's name calls it The Beacon Mountain. Perhaps it was christened on such an evening of prehistory.

The swans were retreating now into a realm of shadows. Soon they would be flying off to roosting waters, and it occurred to me then that I had never outstayed a flock in such a situation, never seen them fly at their own behest, having decided to call a halt to their foraging day. I decided to outwait them. What makes them go? What rituals precede flight? How does it differ from the panic flight of a disturbed flock with which any swan watcher is familiar?

A few curlews dribbled snatches of spring song. Lapwings whooped it up somewhere behind me, heady anthem of spring on the Carse. The swans began to grow restless. There was much flapping of wings, and the bark of crop-scarer guns every few minutes produced anxious responses every time. Three pheasants sprinted out into the field from the woodland on its western edge. One ran straight into the flock and was pursued for a couple of yards by two swans with arched and lowered necks. But a running pheasant is an elusive beast for a walking swan and soon the pheasants were feeding among the swans and neither seemed to notice the other. Perhaps they knew each other. The sun disappeared, the mountain paled, a buzzard called and perched on a far tree, the swans swithered beneath it but lingered on.

It grew dark. The buzzard flew. An owl replaced it on the same perch. A partridge began to call, a silly, slurping kiss sort of sound at five second intervals, shredding the evening peace. The swans became a long thin blur, the individual birds difficult to identify. Suddenly they started to call, tall-headed, and walked en masse, a platoon of marching ghosts, cramming into the furthest and lowest corner of the field so that I had to stand on the car's doorsill to keep them in sight. This, I thought, is it. Any second now they'll be off, seventy-one swans rising above the trees, coursing across the face of the mountain, dispersing on the night wind.

It didn't happen.

What I had not seen was that the corner of the field was flooded, that they were gathering on the floodwater. I could not make out the water itself but I could deduce its presence from the way in which every bird's motion changed from the jerky stomp of all swans on dry land to a smooth, efficient and manœuvrable glide. A thick plantation of swan necks rooted in that corner of the field, and from its midst the flock raised its voice again. Swans will always prefer to take off from water rather than land and I was certain that was why they had taken to the floodwater. Their behaviour was typical of the prelude to take-off, but they stayed on and on.

I gave the birds another hour, watching the rest of the land instead of their huddled corner of it. A fox walked purposefully down the track, a stiff-legged gait, and gave the car a wide berth, staring at it. Nothing else moved. From the swans there was no hint of intent, only the softest of calls, and from my position they were all but invisible. I started the car, reversed to the junction with the main road, u-turned in the wide entrance to the track then paused for some main road traffic to pass. At that moment the rear of my car pointed back towards the swans. For perhaps three seconds a car headlight beam was high over the field, and in my driving mirror I caught a glimpse of its sweep. It was full of flying swans. There are times when watching swans has all the symptoms of dream.

What is there to gain from days like these? A winter grazing swan is not at its most dynamic. The tribal bonds are loosest, the fiery mating and territorial instincts which so galvanise swans into all their best known characteristics are smoored. Yet there are rewards for the swan-watcher.

There is, firstly, the sense of privilege of watching the wariest of wildlife either without it suspecting your presence, or declaring your presence and by patient repetition and ritual, establishing it as benevolent. That repetitious fieldwork, grooving the same path across the same landscape again and again, furnishing detail rather than discovery, feeds and sustains any nature writer's long-term observation of a single species. There is no such thing as too much observation. It is when you wake in an irritable mood and baulk at the prospect of one more day among your chosen swans – or whatever – that you must go again and be still in their midst. It is presence, not absence, which makes the nature-writer's heart grow fonder. So you go again. Perhaps you see the swan in the thunderstorm and it is that which is new to you. Perhaps it is the swan and the hare, the swan and the pheasant, and the swan and the pink spotlight, the swan and the darkness, the swan and the headlamp beam. You win all of these and fold them into your own unique definition of the bird, that personal response of which you alone are capable whenever you see or hear the word 'swan'.

There is also a greater prize, for me the greatest. It is the beauty of nature. I recognise the voice of a kindred spirit in the much quoted sentiment of the Victorian scientist Professor John Tyndall on the view from the Weisshorn:

> I opened my notebook to make a few observations but soon relinquished the attempt. There was something incongruous, if not profane, in allowing the scientific faculty to interfere where silent worship was the reasonable service.

It is a telling word, that 'interfere'. More and more as I watch my swans, I have tried to minimise the interference of note-taking, relying on 'the involuntary impression of things on the mind' in William Hazlitt's phrase. When I watch a line of whooper swans march off into the murk or crouch under the whiplash of storm, or when I return for my tenth visit in twelve days to watch the mutes which nest under the mountain fight the aftermath of flood, I am trying to push myself beyond the scientific faculty into the realms of silent worship. It is all the beauty of nature and there is no end to it. For as long as you are prepared to go again there will be new beauties of nature and new things to learn about swans and about yourself.

A balance begins to shift among the Lake of Menteith's swans in early spring. The resident mute swan pair have decided to make their territorial demands clear, which in the case of this particularly intolerant

Opposite: Evening on the Lake of Menteith

Care of wings and plumage is a constant preoccupation for all swans

Mallard drake in prime breeding plumage

Swans' large webbed feet are efficient paddles and perfect for mud

The Carse of Stirling is a favourite haunt of whooper swans

cob means that even on four square miles of water there will be no hiding place for another swan. He begins by making life so uncomfortable for the whooper flock that they simply leave. They would be travelling north in a few weeks anyway, so they wander away north or west to less stressful waters, urged on the first stage of their spring migration by another swan.

Then the cob begins to turn his attentions on last year's two surviving offspring who have mooched through the winter companionably enough more or less by their parents' side. Now suddenly their escort and protector is their enemy, dedicated to driving them off the loch. Their mother is already out of their life. She is a pale blur on a far reedy shore incubating a new generation of swans on a new nest.

On a calm May evening with the water dark and still, I saw the cruising cob change gear. He lowered his head on to his breast and threw his wings into that exquisitely ominous arch which is the most beautiful declaration of intent to inflict grievous bodily harm that I have seen in all nature. A small bow wave broke before his surge. He swam 200 yards, ran fifty with threshing wings, then flew flat out for half a mile but never more than ten feet above the water. I never saw a swan fly faster. His reflection sped beneath him. He disappeared into the small wooded bay where the adult swans traditionally escort the newly hatched cygnets. That event was clearly imminent and he was about to clear out the nursery water. Within seconds, one of last year's brood was flying frantically out from the bay, but struggling for speed and with none of its parent's fluency and power. The young bird flopped on to the water after about 200 yards, at which point the cob re-emerged, his fervour undiminished, making straight for his own hapless offspring. A fantastic chase began. It had all the chaos of two gulls squabbling over a piece of food but monstrously slowed and magnified. The birds' manoeuvrability was staggering considering their bulk and weight, one more side of swans I had not seen before. The erratic course of the chase dragged the birds towards my shore, punctuated every couple of seconds by the humming thud of wing-beats. As the young bird passed me ten yards offshore, the cob rose above it and by its very speed and presence, forced it down to within inches of the water and an undignified crash landing. But the young bird twisted majestically clear – a hint of powers to come – and with a last desperate gesture climbed hard and fast and cleared the shoreline trees. The cob closed again and snapped his beak shut on the young bird's tail, a last gesture of his own, then his offspring was gone from the loch for the last time and he cruised down to an elegant landing, stood on the water and raised wings high and wide. Then he turned and swam a triumphant mile straight across the open water to the nest and his mate. The nursery was ready when she was.

Two days later, she was. Cob, pen and six-day-old cygnets swam slowly round the shore, the cygnets tumbling on and off their mother's back. It was an uneventful mile-and-a-half, and it took them most of the afternoon to reach the bay.

Their carefree days would be brief. Commercial angling is big business on the Lake of Menteith, and the consequences for swans – especially cygnets – are dire. The mortality rate among the lake's cyngets is grotesque, the price nature pays for sharing the water with people. It is an annual ritual as predictable as whooper migration. Occasionally a very young cygnet is taken by a large pike, but that is rare on a water like this. Occasionally a cygnet falls to a fox. Mostly they die because of man, and fisherman in particular. The problems are fragments of snagged and discarded fishing line, often with hooks attached, the old scourge of lead poisoning from lead weights, and simple vandalism. These throttle, maim, poison and either kill the birds outright or render them so vulnerable that they are the easiest of prey to creatures which would not dare to tackle a healthy swan.

At first the lake's six fared well enough, a source of optimism in the face of disasters at the two other nests I was watching that year. But old habits die hard among anglers and young swans die easily. As the season progressed, so did my sense of foreboding, fuelled by the evidence of past years. The first casualty was in early June, so was the second. By mid-August, the six were down to one. It was not enough that the swans died at the hands – wittingly or unwittingly – of angling. Several fishermen actually protested that their sport had been ruined by the aggressive attentions of the cob to those boats which strayed too close to the cygnets ('too close' is admittedly the cob's own unpredictable and inconsistent definition). Among the ideas which were actively considered was asking the SSPCA to move the whole swan family to the furthest, least frequented corner of the loch. Quite apart from the futility of the idea (it would probably have taken the swans a leisurely half-day to swim back) I confess to a sense of revulsion that the idea was both mooted in the first place and pursued, even though it was not actually put into effect. If the swans were in a position to turn the tables and protest at the behaviour of the anglers, the charges would vary between murder and manslaughter. The best an angler would be able to come up with is breach of the peace.

The angler is there for fun, to catch fish which have been put there and artificially reared to ensure he has his fun. He does not need the water to live – as the swans do. It does not occur to anglers to leave the water unfished while the cob is so defensively aggressive, because that would deprive a lot of people of fun and cost someone a lot of money. There are few more telling examples than the Lake of Menteith of just how loaded the dice are against the well-being of swans.

6

Mountain and Flood

To THE NORTH and west of the Lake of Menteith, all is Highland.
Going north, there is no more real agricultural fertility between
here and Orkney. The first mountains are five minutes away as the
swan flies, and in their lee lies a long and narrow, deep and curving
loch where the mountains and forests mimic themselves in the water.
Loch Lubnaig is much admired by caravan and coach tourism and
frequented by lay-by lingerers, anglers and damnable midges. If you
are new to the Highlands it is here that you begin to recognise what
all the fuss is about, what such as Scott and Landseer and Queen
Victoria saw in the place. Some of the Forestry Commission's most
enlightened work was practised on these steep mountainsides,
although the current obsession for clear-felling is hardly a fit tribute to
the vision of earlier regimes.

The loch's north shore is a reedy treacherous bog bisected into small
bays by the tree-lined thrust of a river. It is one of those dark, deep
and deceptive rivers fringed with alder and hazel, foraged by otters,
and until a few years ago, its gloomiest recesses were lit by fire-flier
kingfishers. The sandpipers still shrill away springs and summers and
dippers chortle through every season, the way they do, and if anything
is likely to drown out their song, it is the snare drum rattle of great-
spotted woodpeckers, the guffaw of the green woodpeckers, the
tumbling croup of ravens, and the drifting lament of buzzards.

North of the loch and west of the river lies a large lochan where
herons stand and stalk in their sixes and sevens, or litter the air with
grey oaths. The still centre around which much of that wild hubbub
revolves is a mute swan nest. I have watched this site off and on for as

long as the West Lothian pond but not in such detail, so that I was aware of its difficulties in general but not some of the specifics. The year I chose to watch both pairs in detail would leave me in no doubt about the difficulties. In contrast to the perfect habitat of the pond, no hand of man intervenes here and both the birds and the climate are infinitely wilder. That year of all years, the resident pair went to ever greater and more despairing efforts to complete the demands which nature makes on their nesting season.

The late July aftermath of it all looks not so much like a nest as a broch in a moat, the product of uncanny labours which I would not have believed had I not been there to watch it. But first, and long before this nest was contemplated, the river threw in its customary and almost dependably annual spring flood. It has been known to wreak havoc in the village a mile upstream, invading the caravan site and a less than thoughtfully sited development of timber chalets. But the few days' discomfort the villagers suffer is a trifle compared to the lot of the swans.

The timing of the flood is critical. Is it before the swans have nested and layed or after? If it is after, the threat is obvious. At best the nest will be temporarily submerged, at worst it will simply disappear. If the nest is only submerged for a few days, the damage may be repairable. Birkhead and Perrins write in *The Mute Swan*:

> Unincubated eggs appear to be remarkably durable. One pair of swans near Oxford laid two eggs. The nest then got flooded by a rapidly rising river and the eggs remained underwater for a couple of days. After the flood subsided, the female laid nine more eggs and all eleven eggs hatched successfully.

Whether they would survive as well in a Highland flood well fuelled by snow meltwater in the surrounding mountains and a rather lower mean temperature than Oxford is questionable, but there is no question the eggs are tough and resilient. All the same, when the river floods, it tends to wreak its havoc for rather more than a couple of days, so much so that there are records of hatching here in mid-July. That in turn can lead to unforeseen complications, assuming the cygnets survive. (Early hatchers are more successful.) A few years ago, the adults were still shepherding two unfledged cygnets around the loch in October when the first of the autumn's whoopers landed. I

watched wide-eyed as the mute swan cob first adopted his characteristic threat posture, then oblivious to the odds which could have
turned on him, flailed in among fourteen whooper swans and drove
them off all at once, and was not satisfied with his efforts until they
had disappeared round the curve of the loch two miles distant. He
flew after them, snapping at their heels every wingbeat of the way.
That was a late flood year in which the nest was destroyed.

  The consequences of an early flood, however, can be much worse,
and it was an early flood in late March which provided the platform
for the extraordinary season I had chosen to set against the tranquillity
of the pond. The rains began around the 28th and fell for two weeks,
flayed by big winds. The river dismissed its banks and began to
explore fields, hedgerows, copses; it obliterated the reed beds of the
loch's two bays, then spread until it engulfed the lochan, much of the
boggy ground beyond it, and every fence, gate, stile, bush and small
tree which lay in its path. The effect was to extend the loch's normal
boundary by about a mile to the north. The swans swam morosely
around the devastation, staying close to the western shore where their
preferred nesting reed beds once were. They swam through trees,
over gates, and pushed into the northernmost reaches of the flood.
They were clearly anxious to nest, but by April 11, there was still
nothing remotely like a serviceable nest site. That night, abruptly, the
rain stopped. My notes for April 13, typed from tape recordings made
at the lochside, read:

> Found male sitting on beginnings of nest, building on a site which
> less than forty-eight hours ago was under three to four feet of water.
> Still quite flooded between nest and top of the loch (lochan still not
> visible as a separate water sheet) and the swans can still swim more
> or less all the way to the nest site. Even in the drier bits the water
> between the tussocks is two or three feet deep. Treacherous for non-
> swans like me, but water has gone down remarkably in two days.
> Impossible for me to get within fifty yards of the nest. Still snow
> on the mountains to w. of loch. Crow challenges swan in mischiev-
> ous dart but the swan turns on it and raises its wings, intimidation
> enough! Cob stops working on nest for an hour at midday. Stands
> one-footed on nest, neck 'laid off' to one side, head-in-spine,
> looking restful, but just enough of head is above back feathers to let

one eye watch me. That eye has not been off me since I sat down a hundred yards away. No threat. Head and neck rise if I stand, but that's all. Four buzzards jousting above the hill forests. Nest site in there? Siskins buoyant flight and call to and from tops of the flooded trees. First truly dry day for two weeks, some sun now, and warm while it lasts. Swans enjoying it. Pen quarter of a mile away, feeding.

I made no attempt to hide myself, as I wanted to become familiar to the swans. I noticed that the neck was much darker than the back and wings, yellow-grey with deep black shadows where it lay across the folded wings like a yard of rope. The pronounced whites were on the breast and the top of the folded wing and tail . . . these in full sunlight. The underside of the tail was brownish grey, reflecting sodden grasses and floodwater.

The following day the nest was finished. It was five feet across at the base, slightly tapered so that it was perhaps four feet wide at the top and two feet high. A cup had been fashioned in it for eggs, a very small cup, unconscious symbol of the fate which was to befall it. It had been thrown together in forty-eight hours, suggesting a sense of urgency. The swans still swam far apart and I had seen no hint of courtship despite many hours of watching them. Their behaviour in mid April was reminiscent of the West Lothian pair in February! They would be later nesters anyway, by the very nature of their chosen territory, and the absence of five-star service from human neighbours, but not this much later. It is possible that the bad weather had acted as a 'turn-off', because they knew the folly of having eggs to lay where there was no nest site on which to build and no nest in which to lay them. Already the hastily built nest was showing fatal shortcomings as a site.

The floodwaters had receded enough to redefine the lochan to the north of the main loch, and I was able to walk, more or less dry shod, right up to the nest. The birds were feeding out on the lochan, fully half a mile from the nest. Even more crucial, they would have to walk over very awkward ground to reach the nest now that fences, gates and trees had resurfaced. There were new physical barriers to be negotiated on every journey between nest and water. Yesterday they could swim over a wire fence; today they had to seek out a gap and swim through it. The portents were not good.

I walked down to the lochan to photograph the birds in a day of glittering spring light. I sat quietly by the edge of some partially submerged trees, knowing that sooner or later the birds would have to swim through them – or fly over them – if they returned to the nest. It was a long wait. The bee-line is not the mute swan's favourite mode of travel, and is only ever used around the nest or in flight. Two lazy hours drifted past in which they fed and preened and idled and showed no interest either in the nest or each other.

I had time to open eyes and ears to the swans' fellow travellers. The shrill giggling falsetto rising from the depths of the reed beds like smoke from a forest clearing was a familiar echo. There were little grebes here too. Tree pipits were in evidence for the first time, free-falling cock-tailed down chutes of song, and the riverside trees behind me thrummed to the small orchestrations of tits and siskins. Green woodpeckers seemed to be calling at every compass point; eventually I pinned down four separate birds, but four green woodpeckers tend to sound like forty. A buzzard was displaying above a corner of a high hill wood, soaring and diving in a pale imitation of eagles, but in the absence of eagles, impressive enough.

I dragged the glasses away from the buzzards, startled by a soft grunt a few yards away. The pen had sidled up the hidden shore of the lochan and was now swimming calmly past me through pools of vivid yellow light, threading a careful path between the trunks of half-submerged trees. She paused precisely where I had set up the camera, hoping the birds might swim into a carefully composed frame of light and water and trees. I rattled through a handful of shots, then stopped to admire the perfection of a wild swan in her wild element.

Trees gathered darkly about her, and the water gathered the same darkness beneath her, but the sun split the trees and shredded the darkness here and there with golden trimmings, a halo round a thin branch where it protruded from the water, a spark at the breast of the swan as she suddenly moved forward and pushed the water aside, a bright rim to the top of her head still wet from feeding. As she moved through the trees, their shadows rippled across her back and neck, and when she paused again in a yard of open water, she took the sun full on her and I never saw such a blaze of white. The cob caught up with her there and put twice the blaze on the floodwaters. I tried to think of something in nature which was more beautiful and nothing came to mind.

Clearly the floodwaters would free the trees in a matter of days, and then there would be no waterway from the loch to the bog where the nest was. What then? Would they fly over the trees to an awkward landing, or would they (as I had already begun to fear) abandon the nest? If they did that, would they try again, and if they tried again, would they take the lowering waters into account? The answers were to be no, yes, yes and no.

Three days later I found the pen sitting on the nest, but looking utterly marooned in a wide expanse of brown flattened grasses, the legacy of winter and flood. The nest by now was 200 yards from the open water and half a mile from the north shore of the loch. I could imagine no worse site for a swan's nest. There was no water, the cob could not see it from the lochan where he would spend most of his time, and if the pen came off to feed there would be long periods when the nest would be unguarded. Ambitious predators, such as a fox or dog or a human, could walk straight up to it. She stayed for forty-eight hours, then rose and left, after which neither swan showed the slightest interest in the nest again.

The main road up the loch is on its eastern shore, and as I drove north on April 21, there was a new architectural feature in the middle of the east bay. I pulled on to the roadside verge, disbelieving what I had just seen. Three days after abandoning a nest she had sat on for only forty-eight hours, the pen was sitting on a second nest. It was smaller than the first one, and built on a sliver of land, the tail of a tiny low grass and mud island which had just emerged as the waters receded. What this pair lacked in patience and judgment they certainly made up for in industry. It was a better site than the first one, surrounded by water, though the best feeding was in the west bay, and if the cob chose to spend his day there, as he had often done in earlier seasons, this nest would be just as invisible as the first. It was also fifty yards from a main road, ripe for disturbances and worse from fishermen and boat-toting tourists. I fancied she would do well to stay for forty-eight hours this time. A week later, she was sitting tight, and had convinced me otherwise. The weather had settled into what would become the driest May this century. Inexorably, the island bared more and more land and the water fell and fell. After ten days I pulled into the same gap in the roadside verge and found the nest deserted. The swans were not in sight.

The island was ten feet wide and the length of a cricket pitch, and an advancing ribbon of mud showed between the bay's reed beds and the water. I crossed the bog behind the bay and sat in the shade of the riverside trees to await developments. After two hours there were none. No swan had showed. I waited another hour. A mallard perched on the nest and sunned himself with all the impunity of one who knows that what was for a few days forbidden territory was up for grabs again. I wandered a stretch of the riverbank and scanned as much of the loch as I could see. It was empty of swans. I turned to follow the flight of a buzzard across the loch heading for the high wood on the western shore, but lost it when the riverside trees intervened. I lowered the glasses and found myself staring through a gap in the tree cover of both banks, through to the reed bed beyond the western bay. The gap neatly framed what looked at first glance like a pair of miniature mechanical diggers gone rhythmically berserk. It was the heads and necks of two distant back-to-back swans, felling reeds and casting them over their shoulders on to the water. Each neck stretched and lowered and felled each reed at the base, pivoted and released the reed, throwing it on to the growing heap. Then the neck swung back for another reed, threw it, then another, and another, and another. The third nest had begun.

I wanted to know the fate of the second nest. She had sat there so long that there must be eggs. I eyed with some distaste the thirty yards of soft mud, tussocks and reedy grasses, all of it covered by a foot of water, which I would have to cross to reach the island. I tried it in bare feet and found the mud impassable. I took off my trousers and put on waterproof overtrousers, not with any idea of keeping dry but to minimise the amount of skin which became smeared in the thick and smelly ooze of mud. In Bogtrotters (a species of light wellies with studded soles) I made better progress, until, ten yards short of the nest, one foot plunged deeper into the mud than before, the other slipped from a precarious stance on a tussock and I was knee-deep and sinking. This, I thought, is a ridiculous way to die. My left leg was thigh-deep before my foot encountered a solid base. That at least banished ideas about dying. I put all my weight on it and heaved my right boot clear on to a tussock. The tussock held, and still held when

I wrenched the other leg free and rose three feet higher in a single stride. But now the stride had to go somewhere and the momentum was forwards, not backwards to safety. I hit two tussocks, then a third, running like a coot, but thirteen-stone coots don't run on tussocks. The third disintegrated and I half fell, half floundered on to the island. The nest was empty.

It took ten terrifying minutes to retrace my steps and regain the shore, two yards a minute. I collapsed beside my pack, trembling and sweating and smelling like the inside of a bog. Each boot yielded a small waterfall of tepid bog water. In the far reed bed, the swans flayed the reeds, their rhythm unbroken, and now I knew why they wore flippers ten sizes too large. I uncorked coffee and whisky flasks, washed my legs in the river and dried off in the sun. I also swilled out my boots.

An hour later, much fortified by the sun and the flasks, I persuaded my feet back into wet boots and trudged the half-mile of riverbank to the bridge, then the half-mile back down the other bank towards the reed bed in the west bay where I had seen the swans. On a whim I crossed to the wind-flayed dregs of the first nest, and was astonished to discover a single cold egg in it. There was nothing to suggest that more than one had been laid, and the size of the cup suggested the pen had not expected more. Had some mechanism of nature recognised the hopelessness of the situation, or had she perhaps laid the rest somewhere else before a nest was ready and lost them to the floods? Certainly a first clutch of one egg must be very rare.

As I walked on towards the reed bed, my thoughts turned to the second empty nest. Was it possible she had completed her first clutch there? Normally a swan lays eggs at intervals of two days or so, but it is quite possible that in that very abnormal circumstance, the pen, too, behaved abnormally. It was unthinkable that the second nest held no eggs. She sat tight there for at least ten days, and a swan does not sit tight for ten days on nothing. But why desert the second nest? Disturbance from the nearby lay-bys was an obvious possibility, and the disappearance of eggs could be simple vandalism, an ever-present threat to the well-being of swans. Yet the treacherous nature of the loch bottom and the shallow water around the nest island weighed against such an explanation, despite being within a stone's throw of the shore, and a stone's throw is all the vile pleasure some vandals need when they see a sitting swan. One Scottish court case involving just such an offence heard the accused say he was only 'skimming stones' and hit a swan accidentally. 'You cannot', the sheriff told him, 'skim a brick.'

Perhaps she was persuaded off the nest by the falling water, fearing a repeat of the fate of the first nest, and already greatly unsettled by it. That would also explain why the third nest was being hacked out of the edge of the reed bed and heaped on to the water itself. Birkhead and Perrins say that they have heard of no predator of swan eggs other than humans, but their studies were based very much on the rivers of southern England, where the predators come in different shapes and sizes from the Scottish Highlands. Here, where the hill forests hold healthy and hungry populations of foxes, and where according to a naturalist friend in the village beyond the loch a swan's egg was found a few years ago high in the forest, above the loch, the slack-jawed gape of a big dog fox is a perfectly plausible explanation for the disappearance of eggs from an untended nest. A week after discovering the single egg, the first nest was empty. I found fragments of the egg 200 yards away on a piece of rough hillside. It was certainly not carried there and eaten by people! Again, an opportunist fox is by far the likeliest explanation . . . that or a dog otter from the river.

Yet the egg had survived undisturbed for two weeks after the swans had deserted. Mists and suns and winds had washed over it, the dew had formed on it and dried off in the sun, the first damsel flies had perched by it basking in bright new life, crows had contemplated it, herons flew past it and cast it a puzzled second glance, a courtship chase of mallards scampered over the old nest within inches of it. I thought about its long, cold stillness, about the swan life which did not hatch from it, about the pointed symbolism of discovering a single failed swan's egg, and something dislodged an old stored memory.

That other mythological world of swans is never far removed from even the harshest of nature's realities. The single abandoned egg was both symbolic of the swan's plight in the aftermath of flood, and solution to a storybook princess's plight in a traditional folktale which is a classic of swan mythology. I found it in a book called *A Thorn in the King's Foot*, a collection of stories of the Scottish travelling people by Duncan and Linda Williamson. The story hangs on the princess's twelve brothers being first turned into swans then, years later, back into her brothers. The second transformation is incomplete, however, and one brother is left with one arm and one wing, and as you can imagine, a bit of a complex about it. The princess's quest to make her brother wholly human again is only resolved after many adventures when she learns from the Queen of Knowledge that she must find a single abandoned swan's egg – 'a buff' in Duncan Williamson's rich Scots doric – and break it over the offending wing. The story catches the moment thus:

An lo an behold she no sooner broke . . . de rot, smelly stuff run down over his wing an droppit on the ground . . . an amazin thing happent – his fingers began tae appear, the feathers begin to disappear – an the wing was gone forever!

Whenever I encounter such a story which leans on the interchange-ability of man and swan I come back to the same old vexed question: Why swans? And the more I think about it, the more I remember that letter from poet Tessa Ransford . . . 'Almost like a human being in flight . . .'

On May 8, the pen laid her first egg on her third nest. I watched her from the hill above, saw her rise and cover it before she stepped down from her nest, pushed through the reeds and swam out into the bay to feed. A few hours earlier the West Lothian pen hatched out her brood of eight. Now the mountain swan was hell-bent on starting again.

'Lady,' I told the back of the swimming swan, 'you don't have a hope in hell.' She had, but she was the only one who knew it.

7

A Sting in the Tail

NOTHING WOULD MOVE her now. She sat low and calm and resigned. Unless it flooded again, this was it. Whatever she was sitting on, whether swan life or a small clutch (three, possibly four, seven days between first laying and last) of magic potions for the deformities of changeling princes, this was her last chance. The wonder is that the pair of them had bothered again after all they had been through, but just how much they were still prepared to bother began to become clear when I put my back to my customary dry-stone dyke on the hill. It was May 15 and she sat tight for the first time. Two weeks ago this was an unbroken reed bed, perhaps one hundred yards wide and thirty deep, and the colour of weak tea. The water where the nest lies was about eighteen inches deep and getting shallower as May warmed and dried out the legacy of late March and April.

The swans began to fell a small clearing of reeds, tipping them inwards. That first day I saw them working on the third nest I climbed to the dyke and saw the first small impact of their labours. When they stopped for the day there was a barely discernible circle four or five feet in diameter among the reeds, a low heap of the tea-coloured reeds on the water. As a foundation stone, it looked less promising than candy floss, but the swans were about to demonstrate how well they had learned the lessons of the rising and falling of the water. This time, they were building immunity into the nest. Day after day the circle widened, the pile rose and spread, and lowered and anchored itself in the water by virtue of its own mass and weight. By the time she clambered aboard to lay her first egg, it was to sit on something which resembled the flattened conning tower of a bizarre and half-submerged submarine. From the lochshore all you saw was the top half of a swan through the waving rustling reed forest; she sat on such a pile of dead tea-brown reeds that her drab and ragged surroundings seemed to tarnish her own wild beauty. From the high dyke, however, with its wide view of three miles of loch, you saw not just the five feet wide nest but the eight feet wide platform on which it rested. The small circle of cleared reeds had become a moat five or six feet wide, and the labour-intensive nature of the operation began to impress. The swans had cut every reed at the base, thrown it over their shoulders, and once there was enough of a chaotic strewment of felled reeds at their back, pushed them into a heap, then turned to pluck one more reed, one more, more, more, more . . . for hours and hours and days and days. The sitting pen then began to shape the nest so that slowly the ragged edges disappeared, and a finely fashioned circular shape emerged. Her reach without rising from the eggs was astonishing. Most of the time, a sitting or swimming swan is a compacted assembly of curves, controlled for comfort and convenience, but when the bird extends itself – to fly or to fight or to flex its wings, or in this case, to labour – it demonstrates size and power, reach and dexterity, all of them to a quite unexpected degree. When the gesture is done, the surprise package wraps itself back into its curving swan guise and stows itself away for hours.

The nest was finished, or so I thought, and so, for the time being at least, did the swans. The cob spent much of his time patrolling the bay, feeding, preening, being seen, declaring the boundaries of his territory, discouraging a cruising party. of a dozen farmyard geese with often comic results. Their flying abilities were minimal, and to watch the cob charge ungainly soirées on the loch from quarter of a mile away was to see the hare-and-the-tortoise myth in shreds. The hare not only overhauled the tortoises, it drove them screeching into a frenzied scramble for dry land. I am certain that on long slow afternoons he would enliven his limitless diet of patience by drawing a mischievous bead on the geese from far off and let fly. It helped to pass the time, and reinforced the notion among the other birds of the bay – mallard, teal, herons, little grebes – that they were there on sufferance, swan sufferance.

I liked to walk down from the high dyke to a shoreline grove of trees, scrubby willow and alder mostly, backed by taller birches, oaks, ash, beech, rowan, and by climbing five or six feet off the ground (which was at least halfway up most of the trees) train the glasses or the camera's telephoto on the nest. I could watch quietly, close and screened, and after a while the small birds of the wood – chaffinch, wood warbler, willow warbler, reed bunting (these used one branch as a staging post in flights to and from their hidden reed bed nest) – would sing and call and fly confidently within a few feet.

It was when a peculiar dipping movement by a female chaffinch caught my eye that I realised she was putting the finishing touches to a nest a few yards away. It was a supreme example of functional architecture, fashioned from moss, hair, feathers and grasses, and so closely matched the shade of the willow bark where it nestled that it appeared from a distance like a blunt growth of the tree itself. I feared at once for her chances. The nest had simply been set down in a fork, from which a gently sloping branch led almost to the ground, a two-second sprint for stoat or weasel; and it was unscreened from above, a sitting target for crows. We became familiar fellows of the wood, the chaffinch and I, for a couple of weeks, until, after a week of sitting tight on four eggs, she was gone, the nest empty, and no flake of eggshell in sight. The nest could be lifted straight off the tree. It was a wonderfully worked thing, but as a nest, it wasn't good enough. I replaced it carefully in case she tried again, but like the swans, she had probably recognised the futility of the site – if she had survived the raid on the eggs.

The second half of May was the swans' only respite, two warm and sunny weeks which gave the pen the chance to settle, draw breath and relax. Slowly the reed bed began to darken and grow green in the new season's growth. Out in the bay, the feeding was good. Life for both birds was briefly restful. By the beginning of June I had noted: 'Water level has fallen dramatically again in the past week, and another long dry spell now will maroon this nest too!' On June 3 it snowed on the surrounding mountains, and as I walked down the river to the loch I was bombarded with hailstone showers which hurt. I made for the shelter of the woodland grove where I watched the showers speed down the loch in small skirmishing clouds, the fizzing hiss of hailstones on water sounding as if each storm was propelled by its own outboard motor. Sunlight flashed between squalls, and the loch lurched between black and blue, darkness and dazzle, and the day was gilded by restless rainbows. The riverbank had been restless too. I strayed too near a family of newly fledged grey wagtails, and the adult male flashed a canary breast at me and scolded every step for fifty yards of riverbank. If he had held his wheesht I would have missed them all, but his screeching was all the encouragement I needed to peer over the bank and see four young birds, perfect pale imitations of himself, huddled on a yard of sand. I heeded the scolding and moved on, past young sandpipers (more hysteria) and saner young dippers which just cocked a head and chortled.

It had been a burgeoning week. Much had changed down by the swans' nest too. The reed bed was now a vivid dark green, tipped with gold, and with the pen lying low, I walked twenty yards from her on my way into the grove and saw nothing of her at all. Eventually she raised her head and neck, and was just visible. The storms had smothered the downwind reeds with preened swan feathers, impaled them on reeds so that from a distance the effect was of a monstrous swathe of bog-cotton. Along the shore and in the wood the grasses were vivid with bugloss, marsh marigolds, forget-me-nots, speedwells, bogbean, ladysmock, meadow cranesbill, and the first marsh orchids showed pale purple hints of profusions to come.

A new black cloud shut out the head of the glen and howled down. Hailstones bounced on the swan's unprotected head and back, white on white, and she raised her head high while it lasted, shaking it often to shed its wetness. The hailstones abated into a brief downpour of rain, and then the sun dashed out, and suddenly all nature seemed frantic. With the sun flooding down, the swan raised her head pointedly to its warmth and in the same instant a willow warbler launched a silver hallelujah of song, as if sun and swan and song had been specifically orchestrated by a romantically inclined film director. Ten seconds worth of nature's most seductive magic was then obliterated by ten minutes worth of more hailstones. The sun vanished, the song silenced, the swan shrank down while the white pebbles fell. The weather had broken, and hailstones signalled a new and frantic phase for the swans, the rains were on the way back, and the cob's leisured ease was over.

For three more hours of that storm-and-sunlight afternoon and on into its calmer evening, I sat on an old tree stump fifty yards from the nest and in the edge of the grove. My purpose was to try and tune in to the swan's being, to imbibe her surroundings, to ape her stillness, to see and sense through her point of view. She was aware of me, of course, but paid me scant attention, merely an occasional periscoping of head and neck to watch me side-headed. The position of a swan's eyes suggest that forward vision is not a strong point, although their alertness and early-warning system for a swan-watcher indicates that sideways vision is acute. The cob was a quarter of a mile away, and from where we – the pen and I – sat, he was out of sight. Warbler song began to chorus more stridently as the day's stormy inclinations petered out, and the comparative stillness beckoned out hordes of insects – a personal midge cloud for my head – and the insect-hunters. Soon the air between the nest and my tree stump was sliced by swallows, wagtails, spotted flycatcher, reed bunting, then more and more swallows. Every short shower sent them all under cover, and every lengthening aftermath lured them out again, and the small slaughter was everywhere in the cool air. The wind dropped to a light but cold insistence and the early evening settled to a flat grey light. The land was summer-sheened but because the light was so predominantly grey and unsunny, the colours of the land seemed to glow from within. Now the reeds held the strongest swathe of colour of anything in the landscape, the boldness of the dark green stems, the daring of the gold tips. I put Tunicliffe's test to work on the swan in these new colourings, and found that the predominating influence was not the green but the gold, to the extent that even the vivid orange of her bill held golden overtones, perhaps because it was still wet from the rains.

She looked extraordinarily beautiful in that green-gold reed bed world, her neck reed-straight when she stretched up to stare beyond it at me, a passing heron, an impudent mallard crossing her moat, a little grebe that swam between us, giggling. Nothing else moved but her head and neck and the wind fingering the feathers of her back and tail, lifting them, laying them down, lifting and laying. The colours flatter her as much as the dowdy old reed bed of a month ago detracted from her. The colours of the reeds seem to grow in intensity as the light falters, especially the gold, one of nature's grace notes. Nothing she does now is without fluent grace, for it is all the work of her head and neck. No movement jars. All movement gels. No movement is flawed. All movement is fluent. The same is true of the reeds as they lean and curve to the tune of the wind. Together, reeds and wind and swan sound a perfect harmony, a triad of nature.

Here the beauty of the swan is a different phenomenon from the winter beauties of the whooper flock or the set piece of the pond, for it is both wilder and solitary. It is the alone-ness of it which forged a bond with me that evening because going alone is the only truly enriching way to watch nature. Hazlitt's phrase is never far from my mind on such occasions . . . 'the involuntary impression of things upon the mind . . .' and only solitude can liberate the flow of involuntary impression. I threw a thread of communication between the swan and me, trying to plug my alone-ness into hers, and cynics who doubt that such a thing is possible should spend a wet weekend with Konrad Lorenz's book, *The Greylag Goose*, and have his ideas turned upside down. Here, however, I am not looking for such intimacies as Lorenz won, for more than anything else, it is the untouchable wildness of the swan which I cherish, a barrier between us which I could not bear to break even if it was within my power.

What I seek is to be briefly a part of her wild theatre, as natural a part of it as my wilderness instincts can permit, and by trying to understand something of the way she bears her wildness and her solitary station, shed some of that enlightenment on my own life. For a nesting swan on a beautiful loch under a mountain is a powerful blend of benevolent forces in my mind and I seek that out more willingly than most forms of human company. It is a state of wild grace which the swan brings to bear on its setting, and while it is preposterous to lay claim to such a thing for me or any other human being, it is possible to approach the swan's world in a receptive frame of mind, be still in it, value it, and by being alone with the swan in it, to benefit spiritually from its silent enlightenment. I cannot quantify the benefits, or specify the shades of enlightenment, although one object lesson has been the futility of craving security and future. To the swan what matters is here and now and today, and beyond that is self-fulfilling, and that is all. What needs to be done is done because it needs to be done. It is what being a wild swan is all about. It is the simplicity of her code I crave in my own life, and the more I watch her like this, alone and still, the more I understand, or think I do, which is what matters.

I watched her go suddenly tall on the nest, not rising, but craning her neck high and anxiously, her head turning slowly as though following movement. I scanned the reed bed with the glasses and found what she had seen, seconds before, a sparrowhawk crossing the bay near its reed bed edge and flying directly towards my small wood. The bird perched briefly, a compact slatey male, yellow-legged under pale feathered jodhpurs, then loped silently through the trees into the dark and twiggy element to which his hunting technique is so lethally adapted, fast, manœuvrable, unbeatable. How did the swan pick him up? She was curved low, well below the top of the reeds, yet something had alerted her to the hawk when it was not in her sight (although it should have been in mine where I was sitting), some bird or beast's alarm I had not picked up perhaps, or an instinct on the wind. I wondered how close the hawk would have been before I picked it up if the swan had not alerted me. It is a salutary lesson. It takes nature to outwit nature.

I heard the stacatto riff of a scolding chaffinch at my back, and thinking that perhaps the sparrowhawk had perched nearby and was being mobbed by small abuse, I eased down the woodland edge towards the sound. The chaffinch was joined by two more, and a blackbird and a robin – these I could make out in the din – but there were others for sure. I stood in a dark group of trees, and put the glasses on a vast sycamore which hosted the confrontation. At least half a dozen small birds had homed in on what I assumed was the hawk. Every time I caught a silhouette through the foliage it was of a finch shape with its beak open. The fury went on unabated for fully five minutes before they tormented their unwelcome intruder into submission and out flew a tawny owl with the pack snapping at its heels. The din receded through the woods. I don't know where the hawk went.

Another symptom of summer, a pair of mating damselflies, caught my eye, a brilliant clinch on a blade of grass. They have the same indescribable blue fire as kingfishers, and I know of no writer, and no artist, who has ever come close to the essence of kingfishers. Gavin Maxwell, whom I believe to be without peer as a writer of nature and landscape, did write a definitive contribution to the literature of damselflies. I never see one without recollecting word for word the last breathtaking sentence of the following passage from *Harpoon at a Venture*:

Everywhere were little dragonflies of a bright electric blue; they darted low over the surface of the water, soared and remained momentarily stationary, alighted gem-like and delicately poised upon the smooth jade-green of the waterlily leaves. One pair, joined in that brief embrace of the insect world which seems so pathetically improbable, alighted near me; there was a whirring rattle of wings, and they were swept away by a huge yellow-banded dragonfly. He circled me, carrying the struggling pair, and alighted upon a lily leaf close by. He did not finish his meal, but flew away, leaving them dead but still joined, a spot of colour suddenly robbed of meaning.

The rains returned, and June grew as wet as May was dry, not the kind of rains which obliterated the land in April, but enough to trigger a considered response in the cob. Instead of cruising the bay and tormenting the farm geese, he spent them at the nest, cutting reeds. He worked alone, for the pen sat doggedly on her third clutch of eggs of the year and was much weakened by her long fast. Every day, for hours at a time, it rained and the cob felled reeds, nipping each one off at the base, throwing it over his shoulder with a fine sweep of his neck, smothering the water behind them, and pushing them to within reach of the pen where she distributed them on the nest. As the moat around the nest grew and he felled further away from the nest he fetched the reeds in relays, throwing them on to the water behind them, then swimming round between the felled reeds and the nest and throwing them again, thousands and thousands of reeds, always one at a time. The nest's defences grew visibly by the hour. It also changed colour. The nest itself was built with the old brown reeds of winter; refurbishment was accomplished with green and gold reeds of the new season. It rained every day for two weeks through the middle of June, and every day it rained he cut reeds, and long after it looked as if the nest might double as Ararat for Noah's Ark, he cut more. When she stood on the nest to turn eggs or change position with the wind and he stood beside her, there was room for at least two more standing swans on the nest. The top storey grew to ten feet wide, its lower platform perhaps five or six feet wider. The cob's idea of a rest was to swim around the moat picking up what had become a small logjam of felled reeds from the standing edge of the reed bed and drop them idly on to the outermost reaches of the platform. When finally he stopped building, the moat was twenty feet wide. It had been an astounding feat of civil engineering. No beaver could have done it better.

Through all this, the pen sat stoically on. She had spent two days on the first nest, ten on the second, and thirty-four on the third. All the textbooks, reference books, guide books and in-between books say the eggs hatch after thirty-five days, but none of them say how having to build three nests and lay three times, her performance might be affected. I was about to find out. Having sat through her thirty-fifth day, and her thirty-sixth and her thirty-seventh, I stumbled across one more statistic – that a swan will sometimes sit for fifty days on infertile eggs.

'Surely not, not after all this,' I thought wearily. It would be too much for either of us to bear, I thought, then rebuked myself, knowing full well that the swan would bear it as she bore the rest of that long traumatic season, that if all failed, and if she survived the winter, she would hedge her bets around next year's floods and do it all again. And so would I, although both of us might need a spell off to recover from our disappointments. I forced optimism on us both, turning a blind eye to her increasing restlessness. She rose often to feed now, slipping through the reeds to the bay for a few minutes. Each time she left, the cob swam quickly to the nest, usually following the same route down the east side of the bay, a left turn, a right turn, a long straight, a left turn, then straight along the front of the reeds to the entrance channel, a hard right into the moat and so on to the nest. It sounds – and looked – convoluted, but it kept a clear route of open water from his favourite preening stances through the burgeoning mass of waterlilies and pondweed. It wasn't that he couldn't force a passage through the new growth – he did so often and so did the weakened pen – but there was a clear sense of security for the cob at least in the open water route.

The cob's attentiveness through these last few days was impressive. I remembered noting earlier in the season how I felt that the pair bond between these two birds was much less developed than on the pond, where the two birds were never out of sight of each other during the nesting season, a consequence of the small and self-contained nature of their home water. Here, especially early in the season, the cob was often anything between half a mile and a mile away, occasionally round in the far bay, out of sight for hours at a time. The shores of the bay were the most notional of territorial boundaries. Beyond the open mouth of it, the loch stretched south for five miles, and – especially in pursuit of the farm geese – the cob would often venture far out into its liberating expanse. But you judge the pair bond by how it performs when it is put to the severest test. Now that the cob had a role to play which demanded more of him than patience and an often disembodied presence, he proved faultlessly dutiful.

On the fortieth day she stood again and dragged a few reeds over the eggs. I stared hard through the glasses as she stood, but there were only eggs and reeds. Somehow I had set that date as a watershed in my mind, a cut-off point beyond which hope was irretrievable. The pen swam out to feed, the cob swam in to sit on the eggs and give them protection (but not the succour of incubation), and as I watched her push among the glittering afternoon light and the heady flowers of the waterlilies and the fire-flying damselflies, none of it could lift my spirit from what I now knew to be the total failure of the swans' year. The discovery of a nest of redstarts in a hole in a tree fifty yards from where I sat was poor consolation, the scarlet dash of the male bird little more than one more 'spot of colour robbed of meaning'.

I left feeling tired and depressed amd bitterly disappointed for the swans as they enacted what had become ritual now. 'Sometimes she will sit for fifty days on infertile eggs,' a voice intoned in my head, and suddenly a piece of textbook information sounded like a life sentence. Still, if she could sit for fifty days, so could I, if only to rule 'finis' under a sorry chapter of nature's sometimes bewildering story.

On the next day, the forty-first, June 25, I sat by the dyke at noon, put the glasses on the nest, watched her stand, and there at her foot saw a single stumbling grey fluffball, complete with black bill, black eyes and black feet. The pen had laid her first egg on her first nest on April 15. Now, two nests, an unknown number of eggs and seventy-one days later, she had one cygnet. That is the way it goes sometimes on the waters of the wild swans. It was my privilege that I happened to be there.

I put down the glasses and looked at the swans, the reed bed, the bay, the loch, the forest across the glen, the mountains at my back; the sun blazed, a green woodpecker laughed, goonishly, a grebe giggled, a redstart leapt from his fencepost and back gaudy as Flashman, a buzzard made a bee-line for his forest nest on wings slow and burdened by the prey beneath them . . . all these were the landmarks and fellow travellers of this cornerstone of my wild year. At the heart of it all was one new swan.

'You clever, clever lady,' I said, which was as profound as I could get.

Yet for ten more days, which took the total on the third nest to fifty-one, the cob clung to the nest while the pen and the cygnet fed and explored out in the bay, the cygnet so small that at times her new world of waterlilies seemed like a maze of overwhelming obstacles. To the cob, there was still a job to be done, that sense of duty to be fulfilled which demanded that when his mate was off the eggs he sat on them or at least protected them. Finally that sense of duty dulled and the three took to the life on the open loch. Behind them they left four eggs, every one a buff.

The nest remained the focal point of the swans' summer, but as the cygnet grew and the family roamed further out into the loch, other birds moved in to the seclusion of the nest site during their long absences. Herons found it particularly attractive. Perhaps the sight of four huge and unattended eggs had something to do with it, but a swan's egg with its millimetre-thick shell is a durable thing, and for all the herons' attentions, they seemed to have the greatest difficulty cracking open the eggs. The soft cushion of the mass of reeds and the foundation of the water itself were doubtless unconducive to making much impression on the shell. At least one heron overbalanced violently in one too-vehement assault and won a muddy drenching before it could reassemble itself into something like a heron shape and fly off to restore its feathers and its equilibrium.

Mallards congregated around the nest too, attracted by its seclusion and the channel through the reeds which the cob had felled and which the swans' regular passage kept more or less free. It was a safe haven during the flightless days of the moult, and neither heron nor mallard appeared to mind that it became more and more foul and dilapidated as the weeks passed.

For the swans, the nest became little more than a point of reference, a shelter from storm, a roost; the squalor which quicky invaded it once they took to the open water as a threesome would astound casual swan admirers who know only the aesthetics of the birds and their fastidious preening and bathing rituals.

They proved to be a wary family which I confess delighted me. It was as though they had suffered and endured so much and taken such pains to produce their single cygnet that they had resolved to redouble their efforts to see that it thrived. Much of the time they haunted the nest bay and the bay beyond the river; the nest bay in particular offered the best feeding in the north of the loch, a thick carpet of waterlilies through which even the adult birds found it increasingly difficult to swim as summer ripened. They kept a clear channel in and out of the bay, in and out of the nest reed bed, but progress through the feeding ground itself was a sluggish affair, like a snowplough through slush. There was more feeding close in to the roadside shore, but that was far from the nest, at least a mile of open water away. Forays there were rare, and mostly they kept away from the few fishing boats on the loch or passing tourists captivated by the loch's reputation for photographically irresistible reflections.

The cob was as discreet as the Lake of Menteith cob was assertive, and would lead his mate and the cygnet away from potential sources of danger or disturbance with much calling and looking round to check that they were following. He was the most vocal mute swan I have encountered, and his instincts ensured that the cygnet would be raised according to the wildest disciplines of swans. The satisfaction for me of that state of affairs was that the adults had not turned to compromise in response to their adversities. In fact I have never seen less compromising swans, and it would be good to think that such a strain was hereditary, the wildness of the upbringing sustaining a wild life for the cygnet when it matured to a breeding adult.

That wariness also made them difficult to photograph. By mid-August my long spring and summer vigil had produced no pictures at all of the swans together on the water. Whenever I edged quietly down to the shore of the bay, and no matter what discretion I could muster, the swans would edge just as quietly away, and my delight in their wildness would temper briefly with frustration. Many a mute swan would have come curiously closer for scraps of food. The fact that I had become a familiar fixture on that same shore for four months made no difference to them. My difficulties were compounded by the reeds. The season's earliest photographs show the pen lying on a nest which stood higher than the surrounding swathe of the previous year's dead reed bed. By August the summer growth amounted to a six-foot-high wall which obliterated the view of the nest and advanced far out into the bay, limiting the views across the open water.

It was clear that the only way to photograph the swans as a family on their native water was from the water itself, so in late August I rowed north from the farm and then let the boat drift quietly into the bay where the swans were feeding just in front of the reed bed. It was difficult to suppress a sense of trespassing, and when the cob immediately summoned his family into retreat deep in the reeds, I was almost for calling the mission off. What did it matter, a few photographs?

I pulled the boat round, thinking I would head off the cob when he emerged from the reeds at the other end of what was a well-worn secondary route for the swans in and out of the bay. But he moved much faster than I had anticipated, and I was still rowing when he thrust a cautious head beyond the mouth of the reed bed passage, saw the advancing boat, pirouetted in his own length and coughed a new command to the hidden pen and cygnet. Almost at once they re-emerged from the other end of the reeds where they had obviously awaited the outcome of the cob's exploration. These swans were not just wary, they were clever.

Once again the swans crossed my realigned bows twenty yards away and I began to let the boat drift as they crossed into the waterlilies and their retreat became more laboured. I considered my role in all this and was examining my motives when, quite suddenly, the cob stopped dead in the waterlilies and began to feed. The effect on the other swans was marked and immediate – all urgency and alarm evaporated and they too began to feed. For perhaps half an hour I drifted in and out of camera range, the light on the water flared and dowsed, flared and dowsed as thick, sticky cloud converged on the still noontide. I sat and watched and waited, and the only sounds were the occasional quiet rasp of the shutter and the conversation of swans.

The birds began to work their way slowly through the thickly fankling underwater forest of the waterlilies, dense as the hillside spruces, in a way which I had seen them do many times before from the shore, for they often spent the afternoons out at the mouth of the bay, resting and preening, or in the bay beyond the river. Now the cob led them quietly away, and I photographed them as they went, setting their world of wide loch and mountain and forest behind them as they went, manoeuvring the boat to change the composition, all tension gone, enjoying the calm hour immensely, companion to the wildness of swans, celebrating their tenacious achievement which for so long had looked so unlikely.

With the swan family far out beyond the bay, I turned the boat back towards the reed bed, for I wanted to examine what was left of the nest. It was a stiff pull, waterlilies fouling every stroke of the oars, but eventually I punted through the narrow channel which the swans themselves had cleared into the nest and its moat. Like all swan nests, it stank, although I was surprised by just how much the birds had fouled the remains of their nest. All efforts at maintaining the structure had been abandoned, and the reeds had begun to close in again across the moat which the cob had created and kept clear for so long. What astonished me was that, two months after one of the five eggs had hatched, the four unhatched eggs were still there, still undamaged, not on the nest but floating on the water. I lifted them out, amazed at their lightness now, and the toughness of the shells. I threw them softly on to the nest simply to record the fact of their survival intact, then cast them back into the water to await whatever fate nature had in mind for them.

It was good to be briefly in that inner sanctum of swan life. How it closed down the rest of the world! I have read many texts which reiterate that swans abandon the nest as soon as the young hatch. Not here. Here they clung to its security and its symbolism right through the summer; here they had overwhelmed the odds, and that far grey apostrophe out on the loch at its mother's tail was their astounding reward.

I considered that season among the three swans' nests I had watched. At West Lothian, two survivors out of eight; at the Lake of Menteith, one out of six, at Loch Lubnaig one out of – at a guess – at least ten eggs laid on the three nests. Four out of twenty-four . . . one in six. It had been a bad season for all of them, but only in West Lothian had it been unusually bad. For the others, that's the way it is among wild swans.

It was an August evening when I wrote these last few paragraphs, believing it was the end of that summer's story. But nature had a sting in the tail of the plot. On the last day of September I sat by Loch

Lubnaig watching the family of three swans feeding and preening around the mouth of the river. The cygnet looked vigorous, slender, handsome, the ugly duckling phase of its growth past, the first swan graces had become a part of her daily ritual. Soon she would begin to practise running take-offs. Two more weeks, I told myself. All she needs is two more weeks, three at the most.

On October 10, the phone rang. A friend who had been driving past the loch and knew of my interest in its swans, said he had seen no sign of the cygnet. I asked for details. He had been doing sixty miles per hour and his glance had taken in only a small section of the watersheet as he passed. It could, he conceded, mean nothing. He just thought I should know. I put down the phone with a quite unreasonable sense of foreboding. On the basis of what he had told me, the cygnet could have been alive and well and anywhere on the loch beyond a fifty yards radius of the adult birds. Anywhere. I also knew that, while there was nothing unusual about the two adults being anything up to half a mile apart, it was unusual for them to be swimming together while a flightless cygnet was on its own, even fifty yards away, and that was particularly true of this of all pairs. Finally I thought I had convinced myself that the bird was growing stronger every day and was probably just investigating its own independence. What was fifty yards? Forty-eight hours later I was on the lochside, searching. The adults were not hard to find. They were swimming in the roadside bay. They were together and they were alone together.

I walked a mile of the shore south from where I found the adults, reasoning that if the cygnet was in difficulties they would not have strayed far from where they had last seen it. It is an accursed piece of terrain to walk. A ragged rough and tumble of woodland and undergrowth has invaded the steep rubble bank fashioned from road improvements. The loch was high enough to obliterate the shingle shore. Dead trees sprawled into the water or barred progress along fickle fox and deer paths, things of fits and starts at the best of times. It was a weary mile, punctuated with oaths. The binoculars snagged on a thin branch, and in trying to free them I first dislodged the branch so that it whipped them back into my face. By this time my reasoning was in shreds. I walked the mile back to the birds and the car and resolved to borrow a boat.

A fibreglass dinghy was put at my disposal and I began my search in the nest reed bed. If the cygnet was ailing, it would be an instinctive place to go, but it was a forlorn hope with the adults half a mile away. I found nothing – not only no cygnet, no nest. A hard week of autumn rains had flooded the place again, drowning the remnants, and so completing a particularly vicious circle.

I edged along the loch's mountain shore. A white shapelessness under a tree was a false alarm, a dirty sheet of paper.

On a small spit of gravelly shore there were half a dozen rooks stabbing at the ground, preoccupied enough in their feeding to let the boat drift within a dozen yards before they flew. I stepped into the shallows and waded ashore where a small burn muttered down a shady gully into the loch and chattered over the shingle. On a grassy shelf of its banks were two dense clouds of grey-white feathers a few yards apart. The crows had been on a few scraps of bloodied bone and feather. All around in the shoreline mud were the tracks of fox. A hundred yards away across the rough lochside field were more feathers heaped in a rough circle, swan feathers, a pyre of feathers. The cygnet was dead.

It could have been killed by the fox, or more than one fox. Perhaps the cygnet was already sick or wounded by a fishing line, a boat, a vandal. It seems unlikely that a fox would have gone in among three swans and succeeded in killing the cygnet so close to the water's edge. Surely there would have been vicious resistance and escape to the open water. All the signs suggested that the fox had found a dead or very ill cygnet, that the fox had been able to remove huge quantities of feathers untroubled (greatly reducing the bird's bodyweight in the process) before dragging the carcase away to a cache.

So the swans' season ended on the loch. I drove past the adult birds in the roadside bay and pulled in to a lay-by to watch them. It was a perfect autumn day, early evening, the loch still, every tree and crag and mountainside perfectly reproduced in the water. The swans, too, were vividly reflected. The casual observer pausing here would see the swans and invest them with qualities . . . exquisite serenity, perfect poise, natural beauty, yet their whole year had just been robbed of purpose. What thoughtless clichés we make out of nature!

I walked down to the shore and called softly to them, the same greeting I had called dozens of times through the year. The cob uttered one soft syllable, a falsetto grunt, though whether for my benefit or his mate's I have no idea. I ran the year through my mind like a film – from the first flood, through the three nests, the toil of the birds to build and maintain the third nest, the wearisome last few days of incubation when I had feared the worst, the solitary hatching, the cob's unwillingness to abandon the infertile eggs, the slow growing, now this. It does not do, nor is it helpful, to apply human logic to the situation. Nature works by different laws, and by and large they escape our understanding because by and large we have set ourselves apart from and above nature's laws. The cygnet's death left me dull and empty and angry, but what right had I to mourn? All I had done was to watch and, having watched, write down some of what I had seen. I played no part in it at all for it was all too wild and beyond my reach. The swans' grief – if there is mourning among swans – will be brief enough. If the cygnet had lived for three more months they would have driven it from its home water to begin the whole tedious process again, but that whole tedious process is what being a swan is all about. It is swan life defined. Most of the time, the process does not work, but it works just well enough for there to be a healthy population of swans, which is all nature demands. For nature is a champion not of individuals but of tribes, and the fact that you or I may occasionally come close by our own standards to one of nature's individuals is of no consequence, other than to you or me.

I shed my depression among the autumn's first whooper swans on Loch Dochart, five of them, and they arrived within a day or two of the cygnet's death. I choose to believe it was the same day.

8

The Loch of the Swans

THERE IS A PAINTING by Frances Thwaites in the room where I do much of my writing. It is one of a series she painted called *Flight (No. 7)*, and shows a pale abstracted landscape crossed by many dark diagonals and one or two horizontal lines. Every line represents a flightpath, the unseen routes followed by birds (or butterflies or Boeings) when they cross a landscape. Some lines are bold and broad and close, others frail and distant, some curve and some don't, but all of them are unwavering. The effect is to create a profound depth of field and to set my mind floundering in a lull between paragraphs (between words, sometimes, on the slow and dire days) about the nature of the fliers. Are the dark lines larger birds or well-worn routes crossed again and again by the same bird? That thick horizontal advancing from the lefthand edge of the canvas deep into the picture then stopping abruptly – is that an aircraft entering a band of cloud, or a perching eagle, or a flock of swans landing on a loch or a field? It is a game which can put ten minutes on the length of a sentence, and I never tire of it. One diagonal, much broader than the rest, is *my* flightpath, and perhaps in the artist's mind it was hers. If I put my mind to the idea of the canvas as my personal map of Scotland, that broad diagonal represents my own journeys across my best-loved landscapes into the wilds. It changes according to my preoccupations, but mostly it drives north to the Cairngorms or north-west past the mute swans' bay to Glen Dochart, Glen Orchy, Glencoe, Kintail and Skye. Sometimes it catches me unawares and flies furtively east and south to Edinburgh, the Pentland Hills and the green scoops and swooping valleys of the Borders. When my preoccupation is swans, the painting's diagonal is the north-west one, and beyond the mute swan loch it becomes a flightpath of ever-deepening Highlands, alighting by three waters which the wild swans and I hold dear.

It is October before the whoopers reach Loch Dochart, but that does not stop me looking in September, scanning waters and skies anxiously like a travelling welcome mat. My swan-watching is dictated to a certain extent by my prejudices in landscape, and particularly watching whooper swans, so that although there are better opportunities, ornithologically speaking, in the east, I incline west-ward and find my swans enriched by the landscapes in which I find them. The sense of theatre again. That aspect of ornithology which settles for observation of a particular bird as the be all and end all, an end in itself, is something I find bland at best and incomprehensible at worst. The Loch of Strathbeg in Aberdeenshire is high on the list of wildfowl watchers, for the spectacle of its bird numbers, but its landscape setting is an ordeal for me, a flat and forlorn place run down by long Ministry of Defence occupation. The worth of such a watersheet for my kind of ornithology-in-landscape is that it acts as a reservoir of birds, a mustering station like a busy airport terminal from which lesser flights depart for more civilised landscapes, crossing my painting on the way. So I go among the small lochs of the mountainous west, knowing a handful which reliably hold swans, and a myriad in the least trampled corners of my preferred landscapes where the chance encounter of half a dozen or three or one lodges in my mind for ever.

If I encounter whooper swans in September, and if the encounter is in a wild corner of the west, there is no more glad encounter in my wild year. I feel like an ambassador for my landscape, and I offer my ambassadorial welcome. There is always a chance, and the further north-west the greater the likelihood, that mine is the first conscious meeting between a particular September swan and a particular human being. Why should that matter to me?

There are two reasons that I have been able to pin down. One is that I see in whooper swans a kind of kindred spirit in nature, a restless haunter of lonely places, an inclination to the northlands of the world (they have their counterpart in North America, the trumpeter swans) and a marked determination to preserve its wilderness instincts and keep a wary distance from man and his works. Often during the long

The mountain backdrop of the
Loch Lubnaig swans' third nest

The third nest (centre of picture)
in its reedy bay, the river beyond

Early whoopers on the loch
caused conflict for the mutes

A pair of whooper swans feeding
on the loch shore

The loch mutes with their ill-
fated cygnet

The unsavoury remains of the
third nest with its four infertile
eggs

Loch Eye . . . 'like a city of swans'

Just a swan at twilight

weeks of watching the mute swans in West Lothian or under the mountain at the Highland edge, my flightpath would wander in its mind at least to the whooper nesting grounds in Iceland, and I would find the prospect somehow more elementally appropriate for swans. It remains a prospect, however, one to put to the test some other spring and summer, but still, my idea of what it would be like has only forged a closer bond with the whooper tribe, only strengthened a resolve to know it on its native heath. A handful have, after all, got to know me on mine. So I like to greet a southering September whooper swan as an ambassador for my own landscapes.

Besides, September in the Highlands is the slack water between the ebb of summer and the flow of autumn. It is neither one nor the other, but lies like a brimful tidal pool among the rock and wrack of the landscape; the best of it wears a profound yellow light and a clarity in the air unmatched by any other time of year. I would rather be wandering wild Scotland in September than anywhere else I can think of in any other combination of landscape and season. September usually puts the first snows on mountain summits, and the first frosts into the Highland soil, and with these comes a tangy exhilaration to the air on the high ground, a bitter-sweet September savour. And it is September when the first whooper swans beat down the northern ocean and cross Scotland's shore. If I am standing on a western beach of south Skye when a small skein of vanguard swans crosses it, I feel thrice blessed – by the landscape, by the seasonless month and by the swans. I know too that when I turn back down my own flightpath the swans will be before me.

It was on Loch Dochart that my allegiance first developed to the almost ceremonial practice of greeting the returning whoopers. They drive down the glen from the west in numbers in October, anything between twenty and sixty in normal years, once eighty, once as few as a dozen. Once, too, a single bird arrived in September and in circumstances memorable enough to lure me back to the same dark shore, in that same heady month, year after year, just in case. Glen Dochart cuts a wide swathe through Perthshire's Highland heartland from roughly the west end of Loch Tay to a well-known road junction and station tearoom called Crianlarich. The loch is small and dark, with a black crag on its northern side and the main road to the south. The river filters in through a long bog from the west, and out through long boggy fields to the east. There are mountain shapes at every compass point, but the place is forever in the thrall of Ben More, a monstrous mass of mountain, a purgatory of unrelenting ascent from the loch side and a reservoir of vast shadows which forever seem to darken the watersheet. The loch's small island has a ruined castle, haunt of funereal cormorants, and when in early spring (later here than most places) the daffodils thicken about its collapsed lintel, they do not so much bring needed colourful relief to the place as look ridiculous, as though someone had daubed yellow paint on a hearse.

It is a place where summer never really seems to get a foothold, and a still September day layers the water with an impatient tension. The month must be got through, and the hills above must have their autumn blaze, but really it all belongs to winter, and outwith that long season itself, it seems to be either mourning winter's passing or anticipating its arrival. It is, of all the swan waters I know, the one where the birds' sense of theatre is at its most surreal. There have been black midwinter days with sixty swans afloat and sixty reflections in the black water beneath them and the black crag crowding down on them. The swans almost glow.

I broke a Skye-wards flightpath there, parked under Ben More, crossed an acre of bog, forded the knee-deep river (found a dinghy on the bank on the way back) climbed an edge of the crag to easy slopes and ledges well garnished with small oaks and birches, and sat twenty feet above an idly drifting posse of twenty wigeon. At this point Ben More reveals about two-thirds of itself, but not the grim north-west corrie where winter after winter, storm-blinded climbers step off and die. There but for the grace . . .

A movement low in the island trees caught my attention and I suspected a cormorant on a low perch but, checking with the glasses, found an otter negotiating shadowy obstacles along the island's edge, taking a shallow ramp of rock at an easy lope and moving splashlessly into the black water beneath the rock, a transition from one element to another of barely believable fluency. It might just as well have been a piece of thistledown for all the impact the animal made on the surface of the water. His head showed rounding the end of the island, trailing a blunt wake which set up a curious ripple effect across the surface between the island and my shore.

I had been watching the desultory progress of handfuls of gulls through the glen, crossing the water at about my own eye level so that I could see in great detail their reflected escorts in the loch. Then, turning my attention from the birds to the otter and from the otter to the ripple effect it had started, one more white reflection appeared in the dark depths of the loch. It was dissembled at once into an abstract computer graphics representation of a white bird by the ripple breaking it into horizontal striations. The reflection became more and more shapeless, elongating and splintering into more and more horizontals like flakes of white slate, and I became briefly captivated by this animated cartoon of nature, wondering if it would regain its true identity before I lost sight of it. Abruptly the reflection began to reform, climbing sharply up through the water towards the surface until, with a glittering silver splash that was as spectacular and startling as the otter's entry into the water was discreet, there was a whooper swan sitting on it.

It was the only whooper swan I would see in ten days of searching from Glen Dochart to Skye and back, ten September-into-October days during which even the gathering grounds of the east were either sparsely populated or empty. Yet a single bird had arrived on the loch where I had least realistic expectations of seeing one for perhaps another month. It had been a half-hearted stop in the first place, and only after much swithering did I trouble to cross to the quiet side of the loch away from the road. If I had not done so, I would not have seen the otter, would not have watched the rippling water, and while I would almost certainly have seen the swan fly up the loch, I would not have seen it land, and while I might have picked up the otter's sunwise circumnavigation of the island, I would certainly not have seen it encounter the whooper head on.

What happened was this. The whooper, having landed on itself and sitting on itself, promptly stood on itself in that heraldically supreme gesture of high and wide wings which so often follows almost any aspect of sudden swan activity. As far as I could tell, the otter, having rounded the further end of the island, was lured back by the sound of the swan and appeared round the near end, laying eyes on the swan just as it reared. I have often wondered since then how that must have looked from ten yards away through eyes at water level – just possibly too impressive for comfort, I should think. The otter's response was remarkably cool, considering it was the first swan he would have seen

127

since April; he sank. The swan swung leisurely round to follow its bubbling underwatering, like a small boat on a bow rope. Then the otter surfaced and stopped, facing the swan which had now turned through 180 degrees. For five minutes, the two creatures circled each other, sizing each other up, the otter making a slit on the water, the swan a swirling wake as she swung through tighter circles than the otter. As I watched, I was aware that my heart was thumping, my throat dry and tight, and I realised then that I was in there with them. There were not two creatures on the water with me as passive observer, but three creatures, two on the water and one on the crag, all sizing each other up.

The otter was certainly on to me, turning away from the swan for a few moments to work the wind with his nose, to dive and swim for a few yards towards me and resurface and stare, then turn back to the swan. The swan caught his inquiry, muttered a monosyllable, looked at me, then swung through another arc to face the otter's new direction. To be a part of such a trinity of awareness was to be elevated briefly beyond anything I have ever known watching wildlife, and I sensed that for as long as the episode lasted, I had shed something of my formal humanness and become something more elementally appropriate, some old throwback, something nearer the animal state. I felt lighter and looser and freer than I could ever remember, so charged with purposeful energy that I might race up the crag at my back without a second thought, or dive into the loch from my twenty-feet high ledge and swim to the island underwater, perhaps coming up between swan and otter and throwing them a confusing wake of my own. The otter was porpoising now, a playful gesture which seemed almost calculated to persuade the swan to participate, but the bird simply sat pretty and swung through lazy arcs on its unseen rope, and watched. I felt so strongly this wild fellow-feeling that the urge grew in me to participate, but it was then that the door which some God-of-the-wilds had opened for me slammed shut, and I realised that what they – otter and swan – were prepared to accept was my stillness. I was, after all, human, predator, threat, alien, and as welcome in their midst as an oil slick. But a remnant of that older instinct demanded an audience, and I stood and moved stealthily down the crag's easy ledges to a woody shelf just above the water and stepped darkly among its small, shadowy trees. Otter and swan watched intently. Then the otter swam to within twenty feet, snorted, dived and was gone. He resurfaced out by the island and stared back, but the whole thing was done, the spell in shreds, the swan perturbed and swimming strongly away as I trudged round the shore and across the river to the car in a black depression. I was angered by my own arrogance. To think that a swan and an otter might somehow see me as different, acceptable; that my frustrations could demand not just stillness and quiet observation but participation – what stupid, futile and unworthy creatures we humans have become, I thought. It will take hundreds of years of reverse evolution to win back a semblance of the animal state we once inhabited. My five elevated minutes were nothing more than a freakish privilege accorded by nature and my own willingness to be still in wild places. If I had not suddenly become unwilling, who knows what I might have seen, what deeper insights I might have won, but I disobeyed those instincts which have always served me best in the wilds to try and be something palpably I was not. Those were the burdensome thoughts I dragged back to the car and the journey north.

Hours later, and in a calmer frame of mind, I could cherish the richness of the encounter, and although there is much truth in the train of thought which followed it, I had watched a small episode of nature which had a quite magical aura about it, and in my own subsequent behaviour I had learned something new. All that nature can ask of us is that we respect its wishes. We are what we have become, and if there is a way back to a closer human co-existence with nature, it is a long road and those of us who tread it must do so a step at a time, seeking to accomplish only that which is humanly possible. The miracles take a little longer.

I carry a second image of Loch Dochart and its whooper swans around with me, and again it owes much to the starkness of the north-west corner of the loch where the crag is darkest and the swans at their most striking when they gather there, bright as domino spots. I had hauled in under Ben More on my way to a favourite stamping ground further up that same old flightpath, in Glen Orchy. It was December, a bright and buoyant day, the mountains winter white, the loch unmoving, the swans mysteriously absent. They had been around in substantial numbers since late October, and I had seen them more or less every week since then. It is a well worn flightpath, the one to Glen Orchy and points north. I was consoling myself with goldeneye and the usual motley of wigeon and tufted duck and the wings-akimbo cormorant perched absurdly on the top of the castle ruin like an overdone weather-vane when I heard a commotion in the last few hidden coils of the river before it enters the loch in that same dark corner. The banks there are high and the bogland grasses tall, so that when the swans take to the river all you can see of them, if you can see anything at all, is a disembodied head among the tops of the grasses. I now saw forty disembodied heads, raised tall and swivelling and heading for the loch. They had been alarmed by two walkers who appeared a quarter of a mile upriver.

Whooper swan response to danger is to compact the flock and become loudly agitated. Head nodding – a particularly vigorous gesture ritually orchestrated through the flock – usually presages take off, and soon the disembodied heads began to nod vigorously, so that at each nod each head disappeared briefly beneath the grasses and then re-emerged, as though a scattergun had been let loose at a coconut shy. But the swans did not fly. Instead they swam fast, and hurtled round the last bend before the loch in a throng as tight as the Tour de France peleton, packed into ragged ranks eight or nine abreast. The open water of the loch was suddenly a liberating force and the birds fanned out, ran a dozen strides and flew.

It seemed that two circuits of the island were all that was required to release the pent-up fears which the curves and confines of the river had imposed. Ah, but what circuits – the cormorant now an outclassed traffic policeman! The swan flock lengthened as it flew, its cries vied with crag-bounced echoes. Following the leading birds in the glasses into the second circuit, I gained the impression of a lasso of birds spun round the ruin. After two circuits the leaders flew down the loch to a boisterous landing, a slow diminuendo of voices, much wing-stretching and preening, until a querulous calm descended and order restored itself.

The flashpoint of the manœuvre I have just described was reached when they were transformed from being unseen and unheard to their explosive and gladiatorial entry into the loch itself. The day's brightness was on the birds and the crag's blackness was on the water, and the effect was spectacular, memorable, magical, so that when the flock had subsided again you wanted to shout bravo and encore and all the other silly things we say when a definitive performance is finished. It is wild theatre at its best, and it must enrich even the dullest of souls.

Glencoe is the most formidable arena of all. I have written elsewhere of Glencoe thus: 'You can stand quite alone in the depths of Glencoe and feel crowded out, jostled by the press of mountains. It is not a place which nourishes a sense of freedom of the wilderness. Rather, it is a place to be ensnared by wilderness. Glencoe is, of all Scotland's wild Highlands, the glen most utterly given over to mountains. Everything which ever happened here, everything Glencoe is famous and infamous for, everything it is revered and reviled for, and every passion it arouses stems from the manipulative power of the mountain throng.'

My flightpath to Skye drifts from Loch Dochart, round Ben Dorain, takes Rannoch Moor in its accustomed stride and enters the West Highlands proper through the portals of the Pass of Glencoe. The modern road hurtles through the glen, rockhounds have carved the history of Scottish mountaineering into mountains like Buachaille Etive Mor, the Great Herdsman of Etive, and tourism and every shade of mountaineering competence, from the sublime to the subnormal, invades the old Macdonald stronghold with undiminishing fervour.

The curious also come, and the history students, for here dwells the one dark cloud which even summer's bluest day can never banish from these haunted mountain walls, a cloud which still pours its own embittered rains of unforgiveness. Here dwells the spectre of the most overblown, overrated, over-analysed, the most blatantly deified, glorified and lied about event in the whole vast and unenviable repertoire of self-inflicted wounds which characterised centuries of the history of the Highland clans, all their peaces and all their wars . . . the Massacre of Glencoe in 1692. Three hundred years later the Massacre is still thoughtlessly bandied around as a diatribe against Clan Campbell, unsupported by facts. It was a vile episode – loudly orchestrated by King William and the Earl of Stair, and Campbell of Glenlyon was merely a paid soldier carrying out orders – but it was by no means exceptional, by no means as vile as many a Macdonald outing against this clan or that. But Celtic mythology has always loved a good story, and the Massacre, whatever else, is a good story, and it has all the hallmarks of mythology in the making.

MacIain, chieftain of the Macdonalds and known as 'The Old Fox', and his wife, forever consigned to history as a footnote known only as 'MacIain's wife', both died in the Massacre, and if you hold to that ancient Celtic belief that you should never hurt a swan because it may be the soul of a loved one, then you can surely be forgiven for reading a little extra significance into the presence almost every winter of a pair of whooper swans on Loch Achtriochtan in the lower reaches of the glen.

Needless to say, my flightpath dusts such a loch. Swans here have no need of grand gesture. Indeed it is hard to imagine what they could do to effect grand gesture here. The landscape is all, and only an eagle curving through the glen's high airspaces does not look out of place. A pair of swans on Loch Achtriochtan is small and incidental. The mountain at their back is Bidean nam Bian, summit of all Argyll, a rearing snow-powed Alp, yet they belong so effortlessly. I have watched them fly a mile into the glen from high above and been struck by how far down the mountain they flew. The darkness of the rock makes them so easy to follow in flight whereas you lose the buzzards, ravens and kestrels against cliff and buttress and mountain mass. Swans course the river and the old sunken ways through the glen, and if you would win a glimpse of the soul of Glencoe, that is where you must wander, down by the hem of the mountains' skirts, and be a puny scrap of life yourself. Wander here, where the buttresses frown down through winter's sunless months and the long north wall throws unrelenting confinement about the floor of the glen, and know that there were times in the populous and fertile eras – in say the fifteenth to the seventeenth centuries – when it must have been like living in a suit of armour. Walk among the debris of that older way – buried causeways, collapsed and ancient dykes, ruins of tough little round-cornered houses which deflected away the noise of the wind; people it with a tribe of mountain folk who lived off the land – theirs and other people's – and have the swans fly their mile of the glen then, passing you head-high at fifty yards, flowing downstream with the Coe and alighting on the loch. Then you can believe!

It is easy to ridicule the whole idea. There are sound biological reasons why whooper swans should find the loch to their liking. It is shallow, sheltered (for Glencoe, that is) and has feeding enough to sustain a pair or a small family group of four or five for a winter month or two. And if winter bites too deep, it is not far down Loch Leven and the Appin shore to gentler Argyll waters dowsed by the Gulf Stream.

Yet the myth-in-the-making is stubborn, and the more persuasive *because* it is Glencoe. I have long contended that the Massacre of Glencoe still gives offence, still wears its terrible aura, because it happened where it did, because the nature of Glencoe's mountainous scheme of things acts as a brooding preservative and a conducive arena for the conjuring of old bloodsheds. If it had all happened on Ardnamurchan of the bright ocean winds, it would be but a footnote to history instead of a claim to infamy. Glencoe is so introverting. In their heyday, the Macdonalds would wear their mountain realm like a badge, and others from beyond the glen, whether they had cause to love or loathe them, would show respect.

Even then, it is not everyone who can live with the psychological demands of such a landscape. A tribe which lived so close to the land, so close to *this* land, would imbue nature with many significances. By 1692, the swan was already an entrenched element of Gaelic lore, and much invoked by clan bards in song and story and prophecy. When in 1990, I wrote the book *Glencoe – Monarch of Glens* (illustrated with photographs by Colin Baxter) and the play *Woman of Glencoe* to coincide with the book's publication, I put these lines into the mouth of Seonaid Bhan, imaginary bard to the Glencoe Macdonalds in 1692:

> I have been watching the swans on Loch Achtriochtan. This
> has been such a hard winter. They should have moved south
> beyond the mountains to Forth or Solway. But they stayed,
> daring the icy waters and the snows, weakening.
> Before the year was out, the male bird was dead. That marked
> MacIain.
> Today I saw a new sign. MacIain's wife, shawled in a
> shadow. Her eye was a hood. The Great Herdsman has
> marked her for a folding, and this morning I found
> the mourning swan sick and dying herself.

Who will mourn a chieftain's wife, so briefly widowed?
All griefs will be for the chieftain.
It is not MacIain's death but the death of his wife
which will seal the darkness over the glen. There is no
other woman so attuned. She is the last of her line.
But who heeds me?
Write your songs, they say.
Keep your darkness to yourself, Pagan hag!
It is the Scriptures you should scan for your truths
not the mountains.
Yet it was not the Scriptures which sent the swans.

Fly then
and with your wings
beat down eons
and where a stable stands ajar
bear your grace within,
your wilderness wisdom,
your swaddled hope
to coarse shepherds,
far flung kings,
a destined child.
Fly then, angel birds.

I have spent six tented days in the winter glen. I have wandered
often in the last of the light down to the edge of the loch where two
whooper swans eke out the last available feeding. A noose of ice
encroaches, and without the motivation of the West Lothian pond
mutes, there is no inclination to expend valuable winter energies
keeping the ice at bay. This is not their nesting water, merely a restless
stopover for as many winter months as winter permits, so fly on to
the coast, to Forth or Solway, wherever the living is easier. On this,
the seventh day, my last, the swans have gone and I regret not seeing
them go. But they have left something, a token of their passing, a
small frieze of preened feathers, curved and upturned and held fast in
the ice. I finger its brittle symbolism.

Every year that there are whooper swans on Loch Achtriochtan
they leave behind the same small symbol. So what? All birds preen

feathers away. I prise one feather free, and it travels with me, a talisman, for a year until its grace withers. What happened to one more feather is more bizarre.

In later winter, the courtship high jinks of the neighbourhood hooded crows rasp around the loch, and a black eye sees the feather in its ice trap. The next day and the next, and all the following days that it takes for a hoodie to decide that the time is right to build, the same feather catches the same black eye. Then a day dawns when the dark wings stall above the loch shore and my watching eyes see the hoodie alight on an ancient path. His black feet tramp down that avenue of ghosts to the leaf litter of the shore and his black neb closes on the whooper swan's feather. He tries to gather others but the wind is a vexing will-o'-the-wisp and he settles for one good feather, then he is up and away with it, and the white feather that the whoopers discarded two months before flies again over Glencoe. It's a short flight to the nest tree, where the feather is woven in among sheep's wool a blissfully snug nursery which seems somehow wasted on as raucous and loutish an assembly as a clutch of infant hoodies.

Yet hoodies are not the most careful of nesters and casualties are frequent. So when one unfledged chick flutters uselessly from the rim of the nest to its death, I see a fox pause by the corpse and make a meagre snack of it, scattering grey feathers like ash in a wind. Then the small gleaners of the same wood – the robins, dunnocks, chaffinches and the rest – seize on the downy crow feathers as the hoodie had seized on the swan's and feather their own small nests as that sluggish spring advances.

So the swan in its apparently careless way set in motion a chain reaction which provided for some of the natives of the glen, and wasn't the figure at the heart of the chain reaction the Old Fox himself? It isn't natural history – at least, not exclusively – but I warned you earlier that if you immerse yourself in swans and their world it is more than natural history you take on, and the more deeply you immerse yourself, the more the distinctions grow blurred.

I am not saying that the two swans on Loch Achtriochtan are the souls of MacIain and his wife, but nor would I ever deny it, not here, not in Glencoe. Not in Glencoe, of all places.

★

I suppose if there were to be a place in all Gaeldom that I might choose
to call the Loch of the Swans, it would be Achtriochtan, but Gaeldom
itself chose differently, and the only Loch nan Ealachan I have ever
heard of is in Kintail, Wester Ross's most delectable mountain
kingdom. I first encountered it not on my Skye flightpath (for it lies
high on an unsung shoulder of the realm) but in Brenda Macrow's
famed *Kintail Scrapbook* of 1948:

> A fine rain was now drifting over the hills, imparting a dream-like
> shadowy quality to their graceful curves and contours. All climbing
> was done with now, and I trudged along among low green hill-tops
> to the loch whose name had been a source of delight to me ever
> since I first found it on my map. The Loch of the Swans – or, as it
> was often called locally, Swan Lake. What a multitude of pictures it
> conjured up in the imagination! Indeed, a name chosen by some
> anonymous hill-poet – or perhaps by the 'wee folk' themselves!

Well, you could get away with that kind of thing in 1948. Though
the style is a bit dated, here is another example of my own theme, that
you cannot separate the natural history of swans from the folklore.
This landscape abounds in names like Loch nan Eun (Loch of the
Birds) or Creag na Iolaire (Rock of the Eagle), and they excite not a
word of comment. But a Loch nan Ealachan is the invention of 'a
poet' or 'the wee folk', and the stuff of flights of fancy. It can't all be
due to Yeats. Brenda Macrow goes on:

> The path ran right to the loch – and I was not disappointed. Lying
> among dark grey hills, calm, quiet and sheltered from the wind,
> Loch nan Ealachan might, indeed, have been a refuge for the wild
> swans after which it was named. It is a long, reedy stretch of grey-
> green water, with a group of islands huddled together in the centre,
> whereon, no doubt, the wild swans nested and hatched their downy
> cygnets out of reach of wind and rain . . .

Now a simple confusion sets in, embroiling language and nature
and that old misnomer about wild swans and tame swans. Brenda
Macrow's book is based on a long summer sojourn, her trek to Loch
nan Ealachan in August, all swanless. With just a handful of excep-
tions, only mute swans breed in Scotland; there are occasional

whooper nests, almost all of them in Sutherland, the Western Isles or the Northern Isles. But Loch nan Ealachan is hardly a mute swan habitat. It is much too remote for that. It is, however, the perfect whooper swan haunt.

The loch was probably named centuries ago, and whether by hill-poet, wee folk, crofter or shieling dweller, none too carefully, nor with much care about the species of swan. Dwelly's Gaelic–English Dictionary defines *eala* (plural *ealachan*) as 'mute swan', and *eala-bhan* as 'wild swan', although the word *bhan* itself simply means 'white'. The Bewick swan is *eala-bheag*, which is fair enough, meaning 'small swan', but it is the small form of a whooper swan, rather than a mute. So it is more likely, perhaps, that *eala* was once nothing more than an all-purpose word for 'swan'. It is even more likely that whoever named the loch did not have this kind of dissecting of his choice of name in mind. By way of further confusion, both *eala-gheal* and *eala-ghlas* can mean 'grey swan' (cygnet) or 'white swan', *eala-fiadhaich* can be 'wild swan', and *eala-dhonn* (brown swan) can also mean 'cygnet', though it probably refers to fully-grown immature birds which are browner than the very grey new-born cygnets.

The scientific name for the mute swan is *cygnus olor*, two words both meaning 'swan', one Latin and the other an old Celtic name, according to R. D. MacLeod's *Key to the Names of British Birds* of 1954. Doubtless *olor* and *eala* derive from the same root, whatever that may be.

At any rate, had Brenda Macrow visited the loch in November rather than August, she might have found it to be *ealach*, abounding in swans. I have been there twice now and found none, but I haven't been in November either. Still, it's a water I have been happy to incorporate into my flightpath's destinations. Perhaps one day in June I will find a brood of whooper swans on the islands and we will need to re-name it Loch nan Ealachan-bhan. But I still wish Achtriochtan had been the Loch of the Swans. Think of the myth-mischief which could have been wreaked by a few hundred years of Macdonald bards.

9

Flightpath to Infinity

THE FLIGHTPATH TOUCHES DOWN in the manner approved by Frances Thwaites, at the heart of the canvas. Skye is the heart of my world, the landscape by which I judge all others. If there is such a thing as a spiritual home, mine is there. From Kintail, Skye is a matchless proximity. From Skye, Kintail is forgotten. But Skye is a big island, fifty miles from top to toe and none of the boundaries straight. Within the countless variations on its central island theme I have my own landscape favourites, scraps of water and shore and moor, many of them in the south and west of the island on the Sleat (you must say '*Slate*', not the fatal '*Sleet*') Peninsula, a few more of them range further north but almost all of them thirl to the west so that whenever I turn, from two miles away or twenty, the amiable presidency of the Cuillin is forever my skyline, my Skyeline.

It took a leisurely exploration of my Skye prejudices one April a few years ago to realise that they were almost all the haunts of whooper swans, edging north up the Skye coast before that quantum leap of mind and flight-style which would commit them to the northern ocean. Just how much of a quantum leap the migratory flight imposes on swans – whether they are travelling to or from the nesting grounds – is illustrated in Janet Kear's book *Man and Wildfowl*, which unearths the following astonishing statistics:

We know the routes taken by both kinds of migrant British swan and twenty years ago we discovered the height at which they travel. Radar screens can detect large flocks of flying birds in the same way that they pick up aircraft. An excellent example is that of a 'blip'

138

located over the Inner Hebrides in 1967 moving south at an altitude of 8,200 metres or 27,000 feet, 2,000 feet less than the height of Everest. A plane was sent up and identified a party of swans at the edge of the jet stream; the birds were assumed to have started their journey from Iceland in a ridge of high pressure at dawn, and it was calculated that they would reach their destination in the north of Ireland in a flight-time of seven hours, travelling at the amazingly low temperature of −48°C.

How can they *do* that? How does it *feel*? How do they know when to go, for such a flight surely presumes a sophisticated assessment of weather conditions and how to use them? What kind of motivation do they need, given that they normally fly at altitudes between say fifty feet and a couple of thousand, to push through their everyday limitations and climb and climb to 27,000 feet?

I have paused, as I always do, at Loch Cill Chriosd on the road between Broadford and Elgol, just where Bla Bheinn, crown prince of all Skye's mountains, lounges rakishly over the western sky, tilting massively northwards, to watch another of those little resting-stations where whoopers linger among its reeds. On a bright and billowy day in early April, with just enough overnight snow on Bla Bheinn to leave your fingerprints in it, I watched the one whooper to tarry there through the morning, and tried to pile nine Bla Bheinns one on top of the other to see where that would get me. The best I can do is to conclude that it reaches an incomprehensible height. Even Janet Kear's Everest analogy is a flawed one, because Everest is a tangible mass in a part of the world liberally endowed with 8,000-metre mountains, vast and unmistakable reference points every step of the way. But Iceland to Ireland, even via the Inner Hebrides, is 27,000 feet above the wavetops, a flight through infinity. It is as near a concept of heaven as I can imagine, to die and have a whooper swan take possession of your soul and ferry it to and from Iceland twice a year at 27,000 feet. I can see the soul of Frances Thwaites as a higher outrider of the flock (for I have always imagined that the viewpoint for her painting was a high one so that she looked down on the flightpaths of the birds), painting with a liberation she never dared dream about before she died. Or perhaps she did dream about it. My painting was a gift from a great friend, George Garson – one-time muralist and stained glass artist of distinction, now writer, journalist, poet – and he was also the close friend of Frankie Thwaites, an executor of her estate, and the organiser of a retrospective exhibition of her work in Edinburgh after her death. He recalled once reproaching her for scattering a few tiny white spots across her 'Flight' landscapes.

'The white spots,' she said, 'are infinity.' So perhaps she knew about the jetstream flights of the spring and autumn whoopers, and perhaps now she has no longer any need of the infinity spots.

The road lips the island watershed and dips startlingly west to the sea. All southern Skye's east-west roads (and there are few enough of them) do this at some point, a rise or a curve which suddenly overthrows or parts the high moors and low hills and spreads the Atlantic under your feet, replete with its repertoire of islands – mountainous Rum, lopsided Eigg, the ocean-going pancake of Soay . . . The road reaches the shore, then degenerates into a rugged species of track. My destination is three miles down the coast, and one of the best three-mile walks in the world is before me, for it holds all of Skye's savours.

It is a schizophrenic kind of walk, for the further south I go, the more of the Cuillin unfold over my right shoulder, so that I half wish I am walking north as I proceed south, and end up walking short stretches backwards, urging the mountains to produce one more pinnacle, another buttress, another gully, another ram's horn of preposterous ridge. That means turning my back on the sun and cloud sorcery of Rum, however, and the sea and shore and moor birds which eagerly overlap in the Hebridean islands and make nonsense of the field guide generalities. So I put the mountains behind me and resolve to return by the same route so that I can drink my fill in the late afternoon or the early evening, however long it takes.

A golden plover crosses the track from the west and stands to command the highest tussock on the moor's edge, black and gold and handsome, and possessed of a single call note which would be undistinguished were it not the fact that from beginning to end, a space of two seconds at the most, it drops perhaps a semitone and becomes exquisite threnody. A snatch of Marion Campbell's poem, 'Levavi Oculus', a golden thing itself, sticks in my mind as I walk so that it becomes almost an incessant repeated rhythm, like the ground of pibroch which lays the foundation for artistry and invention and magic, if the piper is up to it:

> And here, whistling liquidly, the very edge of magic,
> the golden, golden plover
> wheel and go.

The lush and dreamy descant of eider drakes drifts up from the sea, but the sun is so bright on it now that the birds themselves are unfathomable things and the sound comes ashore of its own accord, like a fog. I crest another hill on the track and round a dropping curve to be greeted by a new bird sound, the heavy rhythmic swish of golden eagle wings, labouring and close by, '*wuff, wuff, wuff, wuff*', like a large dog that's lost its voice. The bird has been on the carcase of a sheep which now lies twenty yards away, the sound of my approach cloaked by the rise in the ground. He has crossed the track (my mind's eye reconstructs a handful of shuffling half-sideways strides) and steps off its seaward edge where the ground falls sharply to the shore. I catch sight of him in his second or third wingbeat. There are five more, momentum enough for a banking turn which brings him back over the track, watching me side-headed. Four more wing beats set up a fast glide over the moorland edge and out of my sight. The incident has lasted less than a quarter of a minute. I have frozen his flight at the crux of its wind-cuffing curve, with the sea and the Rum Cuillin at his back, while my ears ring with that tumult of air, the contralto layer of the eider sound, the pibroch of the plover poem – and I almost missed it all walking backwards to watch the Cuillin cast off the night's snow cloak in the warming day. Ah, Skye.

A dilemma now offers itself. The eagle would almost certainly return if I can fake an absence and establish a crude hide, waiting in the manner learned from my friend Mike Tomkies. His fine eagle books are based on more than a thousand hours in such hides, a phenomenal vigil unsurpassed by any Scottish naturalist for its uncompromising nature and its deep respect for the birds to which all other considerations are secondary. But my purpose is to find swans, not eagles, and there are still two miles to the loch. I press on, knowing that if I find the loch empty I will kick myself all the way back until I am consoled by the returning view of the Cuillin. I leave the track after another mile and follow a hill burn through knee-deep heather. If it is the right one, I can follow it all the way to Lochan na Leod. Below me the track begins to dip towards the sea and the vivid green souvenir of a slaughtered village, one of the most infamous names in that litany of infamy which was the Highland Clearances. Suishnish.

> Suddenly the village
> monumentally ruinous,
> only its brutality
> intact.
> There has been little healing.
> Nature bound wounds
> of crippled walls, dressings
> of moss, lichen, blessings
> of snow.
> Other homes, interred,
> beyond wounds, doorless
> lintels lean up
> out of what's left,
> askew headstone.
>
> People wound deeper, scars
> raw still as the day
> they gashed a blood-red wake
> to America.
> The bright green fertility
> of Suisnish
> is a deception, stained stubble
> of a harvested race.
> It is the work of sheep dung.

The lives of the Suisnish folk are etched everywhere on the hill above the ruins, old paths, peat workings, dykes, the scars of many toils, but always when you straighten your back from your moorland labours, the sea and the islands and the Cuillin, and in winter the overhead song of swans, bond you to a home unlike any other on earth. Now it is only the beauty which compels at Suisnish, a beauty tainted only by history, for the place is low ruins on a green sward and has gone wild again. The descendants of the sheep that replaced the cleared families still drift among the ruins and graze the sward the villagers tilled, and keep it green. If a sheep falls or goes sick, the eagles, buzzards, crows, take meagre revenge of a kind.

Every winter the swans return, and bring something of the Suisnish folk with them. Only the swans, though, are given the option of return. The swans are the continuity of the place, seasonably reliable, like a good crop. Pausing on the brow of the hill beneath the hidden loch above the green and derelict shelf, with the Cuillin quiet today, and Soay like a floating raft on a soft sea, and Rum a secrecy of shrouds, I hear the voices, muted brass, lipping the rim of the loch and slipping with the hill burn downhill past my feet. They sound close, but memory has placed the loch further back in the hills – it is two years since the first and last time I saw the loch, coming over the hill to Suisnish that November day, startling a dozen swans so that they flew, and flying, put the white crescent of their flight against the Cuillin: my throat had a lump in it the size of the Inaccessible Pinnacle. I make a wide sweep to the south through mounds and peat hags to come on the loch from the far end, so that once again I can look across it to the sea and the mountains. The voices of the swans move with me on the sea wind, seem to chase after me among hags. I stop to listen, still out of sight of the loch, so many voices now that the loch must be thick with swans. I listen hard, and my heart is louder than anything else. I try to place the sound. Which end of the loch? Forty swans? Fifty? Tightly bunched or widely scattered? I try to visualise the loch again. Where would they feed? Between the island and the west shore, I fancy. The best plan would be to go right round to the mounds east of the loch, crawl up one of these and spy the land. The wind makes a nonsense of the voices, scattering them in every direction. The sun fails suddenly. I look back to see the Cuillin and the sea, but a rise in the ground at my back has hidden them, and all at once I feel oddly isolated. Even the swans' voices seem quieter and more distant. I should stop doing this kind of thing alone, I tell myself.

I complete my half-circuit of the loch, crawl to the bottom of a small rise and listen again. Still the same eddying sounds, still wavering in the fickle wind, grown suddenly chill without the sunlight, still the ragged swan music adrift on the island air. I move soundlessly to the top of the mound, squirm the last few feet on my stomach, and peer over at the loch. Somehow it is dark and pale at the same time, a trick of the Skye light. It is much as I remember it, lying in a high hollow. There is the island in the middle, and the mighty re-emergence of the Cuillin. The sounds are of the hill wind, the hill burns, a far snatch of golden plover, which immediately fixes an image of him in my mind, black and gold on a tussock. His mate, a paler gold, will answer nearby.

There are no swans.

I did all the things that were left to do. I photographed the loch and the mountains. I left my pack and walked sun-wise round the loch, which took, I suppose, half an hour. I startled a tufted duck, just one, and a pair of teal. I put the glasses on a high, high eagle, then lost him as he glided inland. I returned to the pack, I sat and had a late lunch, then as the sun reappeared I took a few more photographs. I did all these in a state of numb incomprehension. What happened? What could it mean? Did I imagine the voices, so hell-bent on my own daft notions of the Suisnish folk and the swans as guardians of the souls of the departed? Hardly. I'm not the type. I became unaccountably angry with myself. Why don't you just *watch* them? Why don't you just write about what they do? Be a naturalist and stick to it, be a nature writer and write nature, write about what's there, what you can see, and leave it at that. *Guardians of the soul!* Crap.

I became the centre of an argument. Two voices were raised within me, each one vying for the upper hand, quarrelling like two mute swan cobs disputing the territory of my mind. I was almost able to withdraw from the thing and listen to it from beyond myself.

Daft notions? Wait a minute. They're not *my* daft notions. They're thousand-year-old daft notions, and maybe older than that. Besides, the wilds are full of inexplicable things – mermaids and selkies, and the Grey Man of Ben Mac Dhui, and half the world has stories about people who change into swans and . . .

It thrashed on for what seemed like hours, but was probably only minutes. Eventually the warring voices receded and I took control of the situation again. I was alone on the shore of Loch an Leod, above Suisnish on the west coast of Skye, and the loch had no swans on it, although I had heard them so clearly. They could not have taken off without me knowing about it, because a flock of swans flying is a loud and spectacular event when it takes off, and these were the only certainties I had to go on. I shouldered my pack and cut a long diagonal down the face of the hill to rejoin the track and walked back to the car with my eyes glued to the reliability of the Cuillin. My mind shut off, but I stopped a mile or so from the car for a drink of water from a burn, and stopping, my eyes rested on Soay. I was thinking about Soay, Soay and Gavin Maxwell, Soay and Gavin Maxwell and swans.

It was Kathleen Raine, Maxwell's great friend for several years whose poetry he revered, who wrote, 'Long ago, in the first weeks of our meeting, we had read together Yeats's "Wild Swans at Coole"; and for those birds . . . I had seen tears gather in Gavin's blue eyes.'

> The trees are in their autumn beauty,
> The woodland paths are dry,
> Under the October twilight the water
> Mirrors a still sky;
> Upon the brimming waters among the stones
> Are nine-and-fifty swans.
>
> The nineteenth autumn has come upon me
> Since I first made my count;
> I saw, before I had well finished,
> All suddenly mount
> And scatter wheeling in great broken rings
> Upon their clamorous wings.
>
> I have looked upon those brilliant creatures,
> And now my heart is sore.
> All's changed since I, hearing at twilight,
> The first time on this shore,
> The bell-beat of their wings above my head,
> Trod with a lighted tread.
>
> Unwearied still, lover by lover,
> They paddle in the cold
> Companionable streams or climb the air;
> Their hearts have not grown old;

Passions or conquest, wander where they will,
Attend upon them still.

But now they drift on the still water,
Mysterious, beautiful;
Among what rushes will they build,
By what lake's edge or pool
Delight men's eyes when I awake some day
To find they have flown away?

Maxwell too was once heart-sore at the departure of swans, not from Coole but from Soay, where he spent a last night in the company of whoopers after his shark fishery enterprise on the island had left him in financial ruin. He too was not above dwelling on the symbolism of swans, and after spending such a night, described thus in *Ring of Bright Water*, why would he not be moved to tears by the great Yeats poem:

When the full moon comes at this season [autumn] I have sat on the hillside at night and listened to the stags answering one another from hill to hill all round the horizon, a horizon of steel-grey peaks among moving silver clouds and the sea gleaming white at their feet, and high under the stars the drifting chorus of the wild geese flying southward out of the night and north.

On such a night, before I ever came to Camusfearna, I slept beside a lochan on the island of Soay, and it was the wild swans that called overhead and came spiralling down, ghostly in the moonlight, to alight with a long rush of planing feet on the lochan's surface. All through the night I heard their restless murmur as they floated light as spume upon the peat-dark waves, and their soft voices became blended with my dreams, so that the cool convex of their breasts became my pillow. At dawn their calling awoke me as they gathered to take flight, and as they flew southward I watched the white pulse of their wings until I could see them no longer. To me they were a symbol, for I was saying goodbye to Soay, that had been my island.

It should be remembered that Maxwell was nobody's fool on the subject of wildfowl, and it was his collection of geese which formed the basis of the first years of Peter Scott's Slimbridge venture and thus was born a great sanctuary for swans.

I have not spent a night out with swans, but I have lingered well past the autumn dusk with them, and that too was on Skye, a high hill lochan further south on the Sleat peninsula, a day of late September, a sudden joy at finding a small family group of whoopers at the end of one more voyage down my flightpath to Skye.

September turns traitor. Wednesday was gold. Yesterday it snowed. Today my panorama – Knoydart, Rum and close Cuillins – is well whitened and flayed by a snotty-nosed termagant wind. There is no escaping the abuse of its tongue-lashing. I have been watching for twenty minutes now the lochan half a mile to the west, 200 feet below, where there are five whooper swans with the Arctic still on their wings. I would like to be closer. I plot a course through peat hags and bogs and unseen treacheries and throw a wide arc to the south. Whoopers this wild, this restless, this newly arrived from Iceland are wary beasts, and I would like to photograph them at their ease, not running fearfully for cover. More important, I want to lie close and eavesdrop, to learn from them and of them. To achieve this in wildest Skye will not diminish the hour.

So I follow my chosen path far below the lochan, then turn towards it blind, guessing, faltering, praying I don't put up hare or hind and give the game away.

Damn! Too high. The lochan is suddenly below me, but all five swans are upended, feeding in the peat-dark waters, and my skylining error of judgment goes unpunished. There follows a hundred yard crawl through hag and hollow to a heathery ramp climbing gently to the lochan's shore. A pair of goldeneye at that end of the lochan could be a problem if discretion fails. The last five yards are the worst, gingering an inch at a time to the crest of the bank. A slug couldn't have done it better. My eyes clear the heather to find four yellow-ringed eyes staring back from a mere five yards away. Freeze. But the goldeneye know the difference between a telephoto lens and a slug, and they clatter their panic straight over the swans. My chin gouges a groove in the peat. I hold still until my eyes ache from trying to focus on the heather forest before my face, until every limb I own screams for the release of movement. Any movement. I know that the swans' attention is focused not on the retreating ducks, now circling high between lochan and eagle crag, but on the source of the threat – my source, my threat.

I dare an eye above the heather. The swans stare at my moor-coloured stillness, and having advanced in their bewildered curiosity only twenty yards from my shore. I raise the camera, focus, fire, a calculated routine of minimal movement and almost no sound – just enough of both to establish a kind of unruffled bugling hysteria, whipping through the birds like a new wind through autumn leaves. The pen loses her nerve, leads the retreat to the far end of the lochan.

While they chorus and cruise, withdraw, advance, stiff-necked and tense, the camera snatches at every half-chance until they settle beyond its scope at the far shore to feed. I have achieved precisely what I set out not to achieve, I have unsettled the birds, alien in their midst. One adult is always watching. It is a disconcerting feeling to have your best efforts snubbed by those wild swans whose approval you crave. Such is the outrageous arrogance which is the badge of my species, to plead for favours from wildness (the language long lost), to seek a sense of kindred spirit newly dismounted from the car with these, newly dismounted from the Arctic.

Yet a few get close. A few have snatches of the lost language. Sometimes you think you can communicate, sometimes win momentary insights, but there is no fluency. Maxwell again, writing of the Assisi-like qualities of his neighbour Morag MacKinnon:

Across the road from the MacKinnons' door is a reedy hillside lochan some hundred yards long by fifty wide, and every winter the wild swans, the whoopers, would come to it as they were driven south by Arctic weather, to stay often for days and sometimes for weeks. Morag loved the swans, and from the green door of her house she would call a greeting to them several times a day, so that they came to know her voice, and never edged away from her to the other side of the lochan as they did when other human figures appeared on the road. One night she heard them restless and calling, the clear bugle voices muffled and buffeted by the wind, and when she opened the door in the morning she saw that there was something very much amiss. The two parent birds were at the near edge of the loch, fussing, if anything so graceful and dignified as a wild swan can be said to fuss, round a cygnet that seemed in some way to be captive at the margin of the reeds. Morag began to walk towards the loch, calling to them all the while as she was wont. The cygnet flapped and struggled and beat the water piteously with his wings, but he was held fast below the peaty surface, and all the while the parents, instead of retreating before Morag, remained calling at his side. Morag waded out, but the loch bottom is soft and black, and she was sinking thigh deep before she realised that she could not reach the cygnet. Then suddenly he turned and struggled towards her, stopped the thrashing of his wings, and was still. Groping in the water beneath him, Morag's hand came upon a wire, on which she pulled until she was able to feel a rusty steel trap clamped to the cygnet's leg – a trap set for a fox, and fastened to a long wire so that he might drown himself and die the more quickly. Morag lifted the cygnet from the water [bear in mind a fully-fledged whooper 'cygnet' is almost fully grown and might weigh 20 lbs]; he lay passive in her arms while she eased the jaws open, and as she did this the two parents swam right in and remained one on either side of her, as tame, as she put it, as domestic ducks; neither did they swim away when she put the cygnet undamaged on to the water and began to retrace her steps.

Then, a postscript to the incident which is pure Maxwell:

> The swans stayed for a week or more after that, and now they would not wait for her to call to them before greeting her; every time she opened her door their silver-sweet, bell-like voices chimed to her from the lochan across the road. If Yeats had possessed the same strange powers as Morag, his nine and fifty swans would perhaps not have suddenly mounted, and his poem would not have been written.

An hour of camera-free stillness has relaxed the swans on my south Skye lochan. They begin to advance haphazardly down the lochan, and the camera once more has possibilities. The cob suddenly rises on the water – he has found a barely submerged rock and, in the manner of all his tribe, proceeds to preen with only his feet and an inch or two of leg under the water. It is a less fluid, less flexible routine than the mute, and I begin to wonder whether the whooper's characteristically straighter neck is also a less flexible grooming aid.

There follows one of the golden moments which is the privilege of the seeker-in-stillness. As his mate approaches him unobserving, for her head is deep in the feathers of her back even as she paddles, he stretches high. He is a particularly well built cob, and the wingspan he now spreads wide looks longer and wider than anything I have seen, a vast embrace. For perhaps two seconds, her coiled form is canopied and quite dwarfed by the one wing under which she swims furled beneath his stupendous unfurling. Then she straightens and seeks out her young, and he is simply a standing swan again, busy with breast feathers.

The light begins to dowse. The one Knoydart peak I can see from my heathery wedge begins to fade into the evening sky. The Highland dusk conspicuously gathers pace at this season of the year, and I think of calling it a day, though there are instincts at work now which I cannot name and never question. They say 'stay' and 'still' when logic and stiff muscles plead for the reverse. I have many causes to be grateful for the urge to linger through the last hour of half-light when there is little to see but the shifting mood of wildness as the laws of daylight peter out and the laws of darkness gather. My glasses are still on the swans, and I am only vaguely aware of a gentle splashing at my back where the lochan bends out of my restricted field of vision. I suspect the return of the goldeneye, but as the splashing persists, there is a change in the attitude of the swans, a muttered bugling from the adults, a stiffening of necks, a swivelling of heads, a slow advance a dozen yards down the loch, a concerted discretionary halt. They stare past me, uncertain.

I can rise on one elbow. I crane as far round my left shoulder as my unswanlike neck will permit before excruciating discomfort sets in. It is just far enough. Five red deer hinds and three calves have walked into the shallows fifty yards away, as unsuspecting of me as I am of them. My low-lying stillness and the wind and the swans' vigilance are all in my favour. I venture rolling over twice to a better vantage point. The light is too far gone for photographs and even my new position denies my cramped right arm enough leeway to focus the realigned telephoto, and my fieldglasses are underneath me. I simply lie, watch, memorise.

They wade and drink and mutter. Red deer are surprisingly vocal when you get close and the wind is with you. The swans, as far down the lochan in the other direction, paddle and feed and mutter. The deer voices are gruff, croaky, percussive; the swans trumpet softly, mellow as flugelhorns, the speech of quiet communication rather than concern. Sibelius could have made something of the hour.

Something beyond my perception may have passed between the two, or perhaps some flaw in my stillness or fickle trickery of wind has betrayed me, for the leading hind suddenly stops, stands, stares, nose working, ears restless. She holds that attitude, curiously reminiscent of the whooper's first questioning glare five hours ago now, and then barks a retreat to heathery knoll. There the beasts pause, skylined and black, as wild as the wind, turn again to trot across the hill towards the last dusky glow of the West.

I lie on. The western sky pales and clears. An early moon is up over the Cuillin. Owl cries drift up from the wood above Ord, and the psychology of the hour finally compels me homeward. The whoopers barely mark my standing now, no more than an insinuating movement by the cob so that he sits on the water between the young and my silhouette. The water is the colour of milk, a trick of the light which has the curious effect of darkening the swans, a trick which suddenly propels into my mind the mute swan on his sunset pond in far West Lothian, worlds away.

My path lies beyond the summit from which I first watched the lochan, so I must first rethread the peat hags and climb to the cairn before the long moorland descent to the car. There is little enough need for discretion now. I simply walk the shore of the lochan to cut out some of the peat hags. I pass ten yards from the swans, my passing marked only by one more discreet shift of position by the cob. He is head-up, wary. She is head-down, but still watching. The young doze shapelessly like floating grey sacks, as deep a roosting slumber as any wild swan is allowed, which is shallow enough.

I pause and turn on the summit. From this angle the water has darkened and stilled, black glass flattering the moon. The swans are lost from sight behind a rise in the ground just above the lochan, but high above the crag, where the sky is palest, an unmistakable silhouette is on the air, a spread-eagle of wings, a slow spiralling climb, a long stiff-winged glide across the face of the crag, then a soaring climb to a second bird, and within moments, a third, beating hard from the south. The three birds – male, female and young female from the contrasting sizes of the silhouettes – fly round each other back-flipping, talon-touching, a mesmeric routine of astounding aerobatics on the grand scale, the tumbling aerial turmoil of a golden eagle master class. They are teaching the young one to fly. Yet this mastery, this instinctive fluency in the young bird is overwhelmed by the young whoopers' feat. Not even an eagle is asked to fly a thousand landless miles on the edge of the jetstream at ten weeks old.

The eagles wheel their might across the sky until I lose them in the impenetrable folds of the Skye hills, but again I feel compelled to sit and stare long after they have gone, for eagles, like swans, choose their arenas with an unfailing eye for landscape, and even by eagle standards, this one must be hard to match.

> That seemingly freewheeling eagle
> over Scafell Pike
> is as free only as the snare
> of Lakeland limitations,
> prisoned and pinioned
> by the dearth of mountains beyond.
>
> likewise that eagle
> wing-fingering the Merrick
> is a bird in a pocket:
> here are no mountain airs
> no ridgey realm, no kingdom
> fit for bird kings.
>
> That eagle striking necklaced gold
> in Braeriach's granitic glower
> has a fit kingdom, but
> being tree-rooted is born
> to that withering forest's
> ultimate extinction.
>
> This eagle of Cuillin,
> climbing,
> carves a spiral
> over Marsco's crown;
> falling,
> splits the spiral
> to the core;
> high-gliding, glances
> Sleat-to-Staffin,

Suilven-to-St-Kilda
and Butt-of-Lewis-to-Ross-of-Mull.

He is King of Bird Kings
and in his Kingdom.

The eagles have gone. The swans are going. I hear their quiet
clamour as they prepare to fly. I see them again low over the hill and
heading for the coast, wings icy blue in the light of a halflin moon.
They may well spend the night down at Dalavil where another loch
lies almost at sea level. There the moon-shadow of eagles is less likely
to trouble their night.

10

Hook, Line and Sinker

T HE PRACTICE OF swan-upping and swan-marking are mercifully all but extinct now, and restricted to a stretch of the River Thames. The idea that it still exists at all is thought to be strange in Scotland where there is no such tradition. Just as bizarre is the notion of the mute swan as a royal bird, a possession of the Crown. How can a wild bird be owned? The theory is simple. You catch it during the moult, you cut a design in its bill, you amputate half of one wing – euphemistically called 'pinioning' – so that it is forever flightless, you say: 'That's mine.' Royal ownership gave the birds social status and, alive or dead, they were worth money. The Crown owned all English swans, but over the centuries (the oldest evidence of the phenomenon is from a thousand years ago) dispensed the right to own swans throughout England, and allocated swan marks accordingly. Swan marks ranged from a simple single or double nick with a sharp knife, such as the Vintners and Dyers still inflict on Thames cygnets (a vile perpetuation of a tradition which surely has no place today) to the elaborate sixteenth-century carving of eight nicks (all inflicted on the bird's upper mandible), four each side, and a band across the centre, a circle near the tip, which denoted the Bishop of Ely's swans.

'The practice,' writes Janet Kear in *Wildfowl and Man*, 'was to take the cygnets from their parents at swan-upping and put them in special fenced pits containing a "stew" or pond, to be fattened on barley for Christmas and feasts such as weddings. Henry II's court had 125 young swans for Christmas dinner; and 400 were eaten when the Archbishop of York was installed in 1466.'

It was not until 1909 that Edward VII ordered that no more swans should be taken for eating. (Incredibly, pinioning did not cease until 1978 on the Thames.) By that time turkeys had offered an easier option for two hundred years and were much more docile to farm. Somehow the mute swan had kept its characteristic aggressiveness undulled through centuries of semi-captivity, and it declined in favour as the star attraction of a feast. As Janet Kear notes, 'It is extraordinary that mute swans – the world's largest flying birds – survived for many centuries as part of the English fauna without the power of flight . . .' Mike Birkhead and Christopher Perrins write in *The Mute Swan*:

> To the admirer of swans the habit of pinioning them may seem cruel and indefensible. Nevertheless, it is probably true to say that the mute swan would have been exterminated in Britain had it just been hunted and eaten like any other bird; it was so conspicuous and so easily caught.

It is a short step from that sobering thought to the idea that because it is so conspicuous and so easily caught, not to say handsome, and confiding, the mute swan has become a target for the worst kind of vandalism – that which maims or kills. We may have stopped killing swans to eat them but we have started killing them for sadistic fun. Stone-throwing youths are the most common antagonists, and if they miss, the swan can simply back off – if it has enough room – but when it is in moult and on a river or canal or pond, it is pretty helpless. There is a good deal of nonsense talked about the ability of a swan to break a human arm with a blow from its wings. It is probably theoretically possible, if your bones are particularly frail and you are particularly unlucky, but statistically it would be a fluke. The incidence of swan wings being broken by humans, on the other hand, is one of sickening regularity. Apart from stones and bricks and bottles, the weapons used include oars, boats themselves, boat hooks, and even crossbow bolts.

Sandra Hogben, who runs an SSPCA centre at Inverkeithing in Fife (it began a few years ago as a modest project to clean oiled seabirds) handles swans in every imaginable state of distress, and some which are quite unimaginable. Vandalism is high on the list of the causes of injury to the birds she and her small staff have to deal with. After tar had been poured into a canal where swans nest, an adult pair and two juveniles swam into it and foundered. A tar-infested swan is something

obscene. The birds were cleaned and released, but the oafs who
polluted their native water are still out there. The birds may be back.
A whooper swan with a crossbow bolt through its wing survived, but
it will never fly again. A home was found for it in a wildlife park at
Inveraray, where there was already another casualty. The two birds
may breed, in which case their offspring may be luckier.

Len Baker, who ran his swan hospital in the south of England, told
his story to Robin Page in the latter's book, *Journeys into Britain*:

> In 1977 I found a swan tangled in a fishing line. We called her Ella.
> That was 615 swans ago and we have released 497 back into the
> wild. Normally a swan will live fifty to sixty years in captivity; in
> the wild the average lifespan is three years, two months. Last year,
> 1980, we studied the breeding success of ten pairs of swans. Sixty-
> five cygnets were hatched; fifty-two were killed. Thirty-eight died
> because of fishing hooks and lines; three were shot; nine died as a
> result of boating accidents, five of which were intentional, two were
> killed by stoning and thirteen survived.

In 1979 Len Baker found Ella again. 'She had been crucified on a tree
with three crossbow bolts, two through her wings and one through
her chest; she died in my arms as I took her down. It was the first
time I ever shed a tear over a swan.' And Janet Kear contributes the
following:

> One incident . . . involved the fastening around a swan's beak of a
> tight rubber band that prevented it from feeding and drinking; it
> was only when the bird had worn the band for eight days and was
> sufficiently weakened that an RSPCA officer was able to recapture
> it and remove the constriction. It has been calculated that out of
> every 2,400 swan eggs laid, only a thousand will hatch; 78 per cent
> of this loss is due to human interference and more especially to the
> removal or destruction of eggs by small boys.

At Inverkeithing, the Scottish SSPCA had sixty-one swans through
the centre in 1990, of which two were whoopers, the rest mutes.
Altogether thirty-seven swans went back to the wild. Ten were put
down, all of them either lead poisoned or with broken wings,
including the whooper with the crossbow bolt. They also arranged

for a very young cygnet to be flown over from Northern Ireland, fed it up, and it is now wild on Loch Leven.

The centre is particularly well equipped to handle oiled swans, but with anything between 25,000 and 50,000 feathers to attend to it is a long and painstaking business '. . . five to seven hours on a single bird,' Sandra Hogben said. 'If the oil pollution is inland, it is usually vandalism.' Two weeks after we met I spoke to her again on the phone. The centre was frantically busy, particularly with oiled seals (a recent addition to the facilities is a seal-cleaning wing acquired with the help of the 'Challenge Anneka' television programme: conservation's benefactors come in strange guises), and there had been another case of a polluted river which had claimed the lives of cygnets. 'Two swan families were affected. The adults have all been returned to the river, but one pair came in with seven cygnets and is going back with five, the other came in with six and they're going back with one.' Swan statistics, it seems, are never anything other than staggering, or shocking, or both.

Many of Sandra Hogben's swan victims are pylon line casualties.

The problems seem to be mostly in bad visibility. The swans just don't see the lines [again, the implication is poor forward vision] and although some authorities put brightly coloured discs on overhead wires, that doesn't really help at the most crucial time, when the visibility is bad. Len Baker campaigned to have overhead lines undergrounded on well known swan flightpaths, but nowhere was his campaign successful.

Even the lowest, flimsiest lines on wooden poles can kill swans. I found a dead whooper swan beside just such a power line in fields in the Carse of Stirling where autumn and winter mists are common. A swan which is maimed by such an accident, rather than electrocuted and killed outright, will usually lie in a field until a fox finds it and the crows come down for its eyes. Those which make it to the SSPCA's care, whether they live or die, are the lucky ones.

Then there is lead poisoning, which in the early 1980s was killing up to 4,000 swans a year in Britain. Much of the problem was caused by lead weights used by anglers which the swans ingested as they sifted grit from banks and river beds. Grit is a necessary part of the swan's digestive system, as it is with many birds. The effect of lead poisoning is to weaken muscles vital to the processing of food, so the bird starves while its gullet is stuffed full of food. A swan suffering from lead poison can be recognised by a pronounced kink at the base of its neck, the muscles so weak that they cannot hold the neck upright.

Some progress has been made. Substitutes have been found for lead, and in 1987 it became illegal to import or supply lead weights of the critical size and weight. Stock-piled weights were not banned, and in any case many anglers, particularly in Scotland, are not controlled by clubs. With many more making their own lead weights, control is a sporadic and haphazard business. Still the swans die, and still they die in unacceptably large numbers. One would be an unacceptable number, but according to Birkhead and Perrins, 'overall, more swans are dying from this cause than any other'. Anglers' weights are by no means the whole story, however, and shotgun pellets produce exactly the same effect.

If anything, wildfowling is a more culpable offence against swans because it is often legally practised on waters which are set aside for the protection of wildfowl. Loch Leven on the Fife-Kinross-shire border is a barely credible example. It is a national nature reserve, and the Royal Society for the Protection of Birds has a substantial reserve at Vane Farm on its southern shore. Whoopers, mutes and occasionally Bewicks winter here amid vast flocks of geese and duck, but the agreement which permitted the establishment of the reserve insisted on wildfowling rights being maintained. So the lead fired from a gun which misses its intended victim falls to the ground and lies there for decades before it corrodes beyond the point at which it can harm wildfowl. You don't have to score a direct hit to kill in a place like Loch Leven; you just won't get the bird you kill, that's all.

One more statistic. A study of lead shot found at twenty-two sites in Britain revealed up to 30,000 pellets per hectare. Usually one is enough to kill a small duck, three for a swan. Many birds which die from shotgun pellets have ingested many times that number. Where lead shot is to be found on the ground, there is usually a lot of it.

There have also been changes for the better. The new ringpulls on cans of drink, which were designed to stop litter by keeping them attached to the can, have also kept them out of the gullets of swans. It was a problem Brian Cadzow encountered from time to time in West Lothian, and many an SSPCA inspector has stories which confirm the once widespread nature of the problem. As Brian put it: 'You can't just look down a mute swan cob's throat and ask it to say "ah!"'

Nevertheless many swan horror stories concern injuries inflicted by the one enduring thoughtlessness among anglers which does not change. Discarded pieces of nylon line, often with hooks, weights and floats attached, are literally murderous. Swans sift them up with vegetation and swallow them hook, line and sinker, and are fatally contaminated. My friend Keith Graham, one-time countryside ranger whose beat included the loch where I watched the flooded swans, once encountered a mute swan there which had a piece of line snagged round one foot and one wing. Each time the bird moved its foot, either to walk or to paddle, the nylon bit deeper into the wing. He was able to save that one. Len Baker tells of another bird so fouled up by a partially swallowed line that it cut through the lower mandible of its beak and severed it. He fashioned a replacement of fibreglass. I found a piece of discarded line complete with hook, fly and float within yards of the Loch Lubnaig mutes' third nest. What if their astounding efforts to produce one chick from three nests had been foiled at last by the cygnet swallowing the hook? What recourse is there, other than my outrage, if such a commonplace incident had happened there?

I can see no reason why the discarding of a piece of fishing line should not be made as serious an offence as the theft of the eggs of such protected birds as eagle or peregrine or osprey. There may be no malicious intent on the part of the angler, but he knows well enough what the consequences of his laziness could be. It would not be an easy law to enforce, but then neither is the protection of eagle eggs, and the very fact of the law itself would deter many from discarding their lines.

Legislation could also insist on substitutes for lead shot, and the traditional preference among wildfowlers for lead is not really a justifiable reason for perpetuating the status quo. But isn't the whole idea of wildfowling among birds on a nature reserve an appalling self-indulgence anyway? Don't we need legislation to give our nature reserves immunity from all human predation, whether licensed or otherwise? Otherwise, the best that our native swan population can hope for is a new generation of people like Brian and Barbara Cadzow with a piece of water at their disposal and a passion for seeing it put to the purpose of safe haven. Agriculturally and economically, of course, it's nonsense. Aesthetically, spiritually, and for the sheer benefit it affords swans and all their lesser-fowl cohorts, it is good sense beyond price.

All this talk of swan deaths begs the most persistent question: do swans sing as they die? Is there such a thing as swan song? Unreliable sources, like Shakespeare (who, after all, had lions in France), insist that they do. Emilio in *Othello* says: 'I will play the swan and die in music.' And the following is an extract of one Dr G. L. Doane:

'What is that, mother?'
'The swan my love. He is floating down to his native grove . . . Death darkens his eyes and unplumes his wings, yet the sweetest song is the last he sings. Live so, my son, that when death shall come, swan-like and sweet, it may waft thee home.'

Swan death *sweet*? Hmm.
So do they sing before they die?
No, says Janet Kear, 'swans do not sing before they die . . .' No, says Sandra Hogben, who has had more dead and dying swans through her hands than most people. 'Sick swans are silent. Remember too that they are very weak, and would not have the energy to "sing".'
Yes, says Mike Tomkies, who cites the following incident, in which he tried to revive an injured whooper swan, in his book, *On Wing and Wild Water*:

Towards evening I tried to feed it again, but it simply lay there with its long neck and head extended over the grasses. When I gently lifted its head, I heard an extraordinary sound.
The swan was making it, a high, dying, humming, mewing, sound, through its half closed beak. It was a weird, high-pitched, almost singing noise which to me held the very epitome of sadness. I had read that when a swan is dying it makes a soft wailing lament, the 'swansong' in fact, but I had always believed this to be a myth. Now I knew, with a sense of dejection, that this was indeed the sound that I was hearing. I tried to coax some more food into the beak, but the swan would not eat . . .

The following morning the swan was dead. I asked Sandra Hogben about Mike's experience.

'What he may have heard was the sound of air escaping from the bird. It's possible that might emerge as a call, especially in the whooper, which is more vocal.'

But the world-wide myth, if myth it is, has proved a stubborn one, and I have found no convincing explanation of how the idea arose in this sentence from a translation of *Travels in Siberia* (where, incidentally, the mute swan breeds wild): 'This bird, when wounded, pours forth its last breath in notes most beautifully clear and loud.'

I have never had a swan die on me. I just don't know.

11

Swan Song

I LEFT STIRLING at dawn, followed that other flightpath north which customarily veers off the A9 at Kingussie and burrows deep into Speyside and the Cairngorms. This time there was no diversion. I noted the emptiness of the Insh Marshes. That fitted.

The mountains were snow and gold, the richest shades of autumn. The roads were empty. October Tuesdays are quiet in the eastern Highlands. Just past Aviemore, I counted my twentieth buzzard of the morning. I stopped for coffee and the view of new snow in the Lairig Ghru, and wished briefly I was going there. But the day had another purpose, two hours to the north. I drove on.

Halfway between the Cromarty Firth and the Dornoch Firth, I turned off the A9 into a quiet landscape of low hills and woods and hard-won farms. Almost at once a male hen harrier, slow and gull-coloured, lifted from a roadside fence. The sky filled up with shoals of geese. I had reached Loch Eye.

A few days ago the whooper swans had made headlines here. Something like half of all Scotland's wintering birds had turned up and stayed. I had driven 200 miles to see what more than 3,000 swans looked like on a loch three miles long by a mile wide. The answer was – wall to wall.

I parked a discreet distance from the loch, and as soon as I stepped from the car the sound of the unseen loch was overwhelming. It was not loud so much as impenetrable, a thing of layered depths, so that no individual voice was discernible.

I walked through trees to a boggy shore, parted last leaves and saw the loch for the first time. My mind had fixed on the idea of a

162

watersheet smothered in swans. What I had not been prepared for was almost as many mute swans as whooper swans, several times as many geese, and (to me, at least) uncountable hordes of duck which, I learned later, included 50,000 wigeon. The gathering was the result of a particularly vigorous growth of a pondweed called ruppia. The loch has always been renowned as a whooper gathering haunt, but this year's bounties had far surpassed previous totals.

How did they know?

What secret communication lured so many birds here at once, knowing the feeding would be so good?

The loch was like a city of swans. In every direction, and as far as I could see across the water, swans fed and loafed and preened and fought and bickered and blethered and took off and landed and dozed and woke and startled and calmed down. And all the time the air was a confused Babel of voices, every shade of whooper brassiness, every snort and grunt and soft shriek of the mute swan's repertoire. Ear-splitting wigeon whistles went off like rockets, dozens at a time, and every other second, geese gabbled in clouds, rising and falling, off and on the water. Harriers and sparrowhawks cruised the shores and shallows, doubtless attracted by the prospect of finding injured or sick young birds in all that press of wildfowl.

Swans flew. They flew in short sorties across the water, a few hundred yards at a time. They flew in angry charges which barely left the water. They flew in wide circuits of the loch. They flew in from the fields, or out to the fields. They flew in tight arrowheads of three at a time, or in twos and ones. They flew in long low skeins of ten or twenty or fifty, forging an unswerving route above the heads of the swimming masses reminiscent of sea-going gannets. They banked before the shoreline trees or heaved up over them. Away, and away across the water, swans flew in every direction, for every conceivable and inconceivable purpose. To latch on to one flight in the glasses and follow it was to cross the path of a dozen, twenty, fifty other flights at any one moment. Finding a focal point was like trying to focus on one straw in a haystack. Everything was a focal point, but only for as long as you could resist every other distraction which filled the glasses. The telescope only cut down the number of distractions.

I let the camera gorge itself, and eventually settled to watch and wonder, letting the whole grey and white spectacle wash over me. I stayed for half a day. Dusk brought no visible let-up in the pace of activity, no quietening of the massed voices, no lessening of the spectacle.

A buzzard crossed my shore, high and crying, and paused to circle three times. How I envied that bird at that moment. To be able to soar to say 300 feet above the water and hover there, looking down . . . that would be something.

Yes, there is a swansong. It is the wild music of 5,000 swan throats underscored by geese and wigeon. It celebrates not death but life, swans' life, and my own life for the way it has been enriched by swans.

Epilogue

IT IS THE FIRST week of April. On the hill above Loch Lubnaig it feels warm for the first time this year, but reality is that it is only too mild to snow again. In the deepest recesses of the pockets of my polar jacket, my hands are bunched for warmth. A new nesting season is under way. After the most insipid of winters a bludgeon of hard, cold rains and blizzards has just ended. Through it all, I have surfaced occasionally to traipse round my nearest swan haunts, checking progress, and lack of it. Both are appropriate.

On the farm pond, the pen showed her first interest in the nest island in the first week of February. The Cadzows saw her and the traditional bale of straw was supplied the next day. By mid–March she was laying and by April she was sitting. The cob responded to last year's eerie malevolent conspiracy by tolerating the presence of the two surviving young well into February. It is the latest date I have known, and surely a response to the exceptional circumstances they had to endure. There will be no accident this year, at least, and the benevolent forces have the upper hand again. Even the vile weather of the past two weeks has been thwarted.

At the Lake of Menteith, too, a curious situation has developed. Last year's solitary survivor mopes dowdily alone. In the past week, three more young swans have appeared and lingered, probably from a small loch to the east hidden among high fields which I discovered late last year, complete with fully fledged brood of three. They keep together here and shun the company of the Lake-born swan. It is an uncommonly peaceful spring water because the adult mutes have vanished. Anything could have happened, of course, but I remember the anger of some anglers here last year at the cob's aggression, and I wonder, darkly.

The whoopers have also gone, but it is their time to go.

The fields of the Carse are quiet too, or at least as quiet as they can be with the influx of curlew and lapwings and their kin. But the field where a whooper flock of between twenty and forty stayed from early January until last week is empty. The goose hordes are dwindling. Whooper numbers hereabouts have been low this winter, and there have been no Bewicks at all, but two weeks ago, the day before the weather broke, I returned from a two-day trip to the Cairngorms and found the Insh Marshes awash with floodwaters and well stocked with whoopers. From a lay-by on the A9 I counted ninety in desultory gatherings far across the Marshes, and there could easily have been two or three times that number. The birds are drifting north. Three weeks hence, the Marshes will be as empty of swans as the Carse fields are now, and a new balance in the whoopers' life cycle will have been tipped irrevocably. The quiet Bewicks are ahead of them, flighting up the northern seas for Arctic Scandinavia and Russia.

Now on Loch Lubnaig there is precious little evidence of a new swan season. Through the winter I paused here only briefly, usually on journeys elsewhere. Today I linger above the nest bay, my back feeling the familiar contours of the dry-stone dyke. The floods were early again. They were bad at the start of March, and no sooner had they begun to abate in a semblance of illusory spring than winter coughed up a bad joke, smothered the mountains in its heaviest snowfalls and blurred the loch shore for a week in a sleety haze. Then the snows melted and the river gorged again, bloated and uncoiled.

I saw the mutes harry a passing flotilla of six whoopers in February, but now there is no scrap of serviceable land at their disposal and they spend much of their time far apart.

It is the third week of April. The waters have receded, and in their place they have left hope. The swans, it now transpires, *have* been waiting. At last they have begun to build again, and they have chosen the reed bed in the west bay under the mountain. This time, instead of it being their third choice, it is their first, and this despite all the received wisdom of many sources that mute swans will almost always return to a traditional site, no matter how unsuitable. Yet all traditional sites must have been new once, and perhaps I have seen a new site establish its tradition. This pair seem to have learned the lessons of their last disastrous year, and the portents are good. There has been no premature laying this time in hastily built and hastily abandoned nests. With luck, and with all the nest-building skills which they finally showed last year on their third nest, there is time, this time, to get it right.

All they need now is a spell of reasonably dry weather and the full co-operation of nature. They deserve nothing less.

Select Bibliography

Baxter, Colin and Crumley, Jim, *Glencoe, Monarch of Glens*, Colin Baxter, 1990.

Birkhead, Mike and Perrins, Christopher, *The Mute Swan*, Croom Helm, 1986.

Brockie, Keith, *Wildlife Sketchbook*, Dent, 1981.

Cusa, Noel, *Tunnicliffe's Birdlife*, Clive Holloway, 1985.

Gordon, Seton, *The Land of the Hills and Glens*, Cassells, 1920.

Hunter, James and Maclean, Cailean, *Skye, The Island*, Mainstream, 1986.

Kear, Janet, *Man and Wildfowl*, T. and A. D. Poyser, 1990.

Macrow, Brenda, *Kintail Scrapbook*, Oliver and Boyd, 1948.

Maxwell, Gavin, *Ring of Bright Water*, Longmans Green, 1960; and *Harpoon at a Venture*, Rupert Hart-Davis, 1952.

O'Connor, Ulick, *The Yeats Companion*, Mandarin, 1990.

Raine, Kathleen, *The Lion's Mouth*, Hamish Hamilton, 1977.

Thom, Valerie, *Birds in Scotland*, T. and A. D. Poyser, 1985.

Tomkies, Mike, *Out of the Wild*, Jonathan Cape, 1985; and *On Wing and Wild Water*, Jonathan Cape, 1987.

Williamson, Duncan and Linda, *A Thorn in the King's Foot*, Penguin, 1987.